PLAYING IN PARADISE

N.K. CHAVUSH

N.K.C & SON

A special thanks: Marion E. Stuart for the editing, proofreading and helping with the research. I couldn't have done it without you!
David Stuart for the additional proofreading.
Dev Parmar, for an extra insight into the world of football politics.
Olkan Ergüner for the front cover photo and C.Cem Şimşek for the author photo.
My wife, Simay, for being so supportive of this novel.

1

ISBN 978-1-5272-6486-1

N.K.C & Son paperback

*

Also available in eBook format.

*

N.K. CHAVUSH was born in London. He went to school in Somerset and then later to university in Canterbury, where he graduated with a B.Sc (hons) degree in radiography.

He currently resides in Cyprus, with his wife, son and daughter. His first published piece of work is the first book of the Anto series, Curse of the Hidden City.

www.nkchavush.com

facebook.com/nkchavush

twitter.com/nkchavush

instagram.com/n.k.chavush_books_and _novels

For my family

1

August 24th

OPENING my eyes, I try to focus on the ceiling, but the light is too bright and burns, so I close them again.

'Can you hear me, Andrew?' asks a man's voice.

Agonising pains shoot through my left leg down to my foot. I try to remember where the hell I am, as everything's a blur. I force myself to talk, but my mouth feels extremely dry. An attractive young lady in all white materialises leaning towards me- it's happened- I must have died, somehow made it to heaven and being greeted by an angel, but unfortunately not. She's a nurse forcing a straw between my sore lips, through which I do my best to suck up some water from a paper cup. It's warm and tastes vulgar.

'*Andrew*… my name is Mr. Matthew Green. I'm the surgeon who performed your operation. It went surprisingly well. Your lower leg will be in a cast for a while. Then obviously, later on, you'll need physiotherapy,' says the man's voice.

'I'm sorry, Andrew. I truly am,' another voice cuts in, this one familiar.

I slowly turn my head and see Lewis Orland, my agent standing by the window watching me.

I don't say anything.

'It was a nasty foul. He got given red… obviously,' he waits for a moment and adds. 'Gotta five-match ban too.'

It all comes back to me now- the much-awaited opening game of the season. Although there were no goals, we kept the majority of the possession of the ball and forced them to defend. Just as I was about to take a shot at an open goal, I felt a crack vibrating through my body, followed by excruciating pains shooting up and down my leg. After that- I can't say I remember much, but a lot of swearing and angry exchange of words- and then nothing. It all went blank. Anyway, in no way do Orland's words comfort me, and I feel a sudden rush of anger.

'That's good to know,' I cough out. 'He gets given a five-game rest. And I'm probably out for the entire season!'

'Try and relax please, Andrew, you also suffered a concussion,' warns Mr. Green.

'How?' I ask.

'You got accidentally kicked in the head on the way down,' says Orland. 'Listen, I know how stressful injuries can be, but we'll figure somethin' out. Let me talk to the manager. Or even the chairman. For the time being, you'll have to rest and heal, Andy.'

'Give it a break, Lewis! It was the first game of the season! The transfer window doesn't close for another month. Look how Jon Fabien was treated last year.'

'Fabien was French. I'll talk to them tomorrow, I promise. Just make sure your phone is on and get plenty of rest. You're on strong painkillers.'

He heads for the door and glances at me, 'Can I get you anything?' he says hurriedly.

I half-heartedly shake my head. He tells me to call if I do, then leaves.

'I'm also sorry about what happened,' says Mr. Green. 'Especially being a Hatter's fan.'

'What was the final score?' I ask, my head feeling like it's going to split open.

'We got a one-nil win,' he says proudly.

'So, when will I be able to play again?'

He pauses for a moment. 'Probably around November, but everyone's different.'

'That's too long.'

'You've got a fractured fibula. Needs time to heal.'

On his way out, Mr. Green says that he'll be back to check up on me in the morning.

A couple of minutes later there is a knock at the door. In walks Jessie Fell, my fiancée. I notice she is teary-eyed, so I try and raise a smile as she approaches the bed.

'My poor baby,' she says sympathetically.

'Hey babe,' I manage.

I notice three shopping bags hanging from her hands. Yes, three of her favourite brands- also the most expensive with overly inflated prices. Even when I'm in surgery, it won't stop her from drying out my credit cards.

'Where have you been?' I ask, staring up at the ceiling.

'Well, I felt so sad and vulnerable when they rushed you into surgery that I needed something to cheer me up,' she explains with her childish voice.

Really? That's a new one. Maybe if something worse were to happen to me then you'd buy the entire shop, I keep that thought to myself as I'm in no place for a full-blown argument.

'Anyway, I have to go,' she says, turning back towards the door.

'But you've just got here.'

'I just remembered Cuddles needs feeding. Can you believe they wouldn't allow her up here!'

Ah yes, Cuddles. Her little Chihuahua that always gets more attention than I do.

'That's surprising,' I say.

'I'll be back soon, baby. Or maybe they'll let you out before then,' she says, blowing me a flying kiss, and before I know it, she's out the door.

The nurse scribbles something on the clipboard then hangs it at the end of the bed. She looks up at me with her large blue eyes, smiles, and says, 'Mr. Ashford, if you need anything, press on the orange button.'

I let out a half-hearted 'Thanks,' while staring out of the window towards the brick wall of the building next door.

After four miserable days at the hospital, Mr. Green signs for my discharge, reminding me I'll need physiotherapy in a week and books me an appointment at his surgery for next Monday.

Lewis pushes me through the car park and helps me into the passenger seat of his old grey Honda. He puts the wheelchair into the back and suitcase into the boot. We get caught up in the rush hour traffic, which is fine after days of being stuck in the hospital. He forces a conversation to fill in the silences, but I'm not feeling sociable.

'At least the weather is still nice,' he says, with a chirpy voice.

'Yeah,' I breathe.

'Any of the boys come down to see you?'

'A few of them have.'

'Why's that bastard bloody trying to cut in? Stupid idiot!' he heaves angrily, 'There's a flippin' queue 'ere mate!'

After the pointless bit of road rage, he turns his attention back on me.

'Andy mate, there's no easy way of sayin' this.'

Here we go. The bad news, I'd been expecting. It's always been this way in the sports world. All that sympathy and the '*you'll pull through*' comments- then they pull the plug. I don't blame the clubs either. I mean, who wants a useless athlete in their team?

In silence, I listen to what Lewis has to say. He's been my agent for fifteen years, and I owe him for that. On the way, there have been highs and lows, but none as low as this.

'The landlord has sent a notice. He's selling the property. Unfortunately, the new buyers aren't interested in renting,' he explains.

'Well, that's easy. I'll move into another,' I say.

'I spoke to the club, and all the other accommodations are full. Unless you're a regular in the squad every week, they won't finance any accommodations outside their agreement. Not even a studio.'

I start feeling flushed.

'So where am I supposed to stay, Lewis?' I ask.

He's silent for a moment. 'I'll work something out,' he mumbles.

His face lights up after a minute and says, 'How about your mums for a couple of months?'

I don't answer.

My mother lives up north. If I were to stay with her for a few months, I would be distancing myself from the club, which could eventually spell the end of my career. Jessie would undoubtedly be against the idea. I try to think of other alternatives. At the age of twenty-six, all I know is football. A change of career would be drastic at this stage.

Lewis' annoying old-fashioned ring tone loudly jingles in my ear.

'It's Stu from the club!' he says, answering it.

'Hello? Stuart! Good, you?' he then turns and looks at me with a slight smile.

'*Already?* That was very quick! No, I haven't mentioned anything yet. Ok, we'll be over in about forty minutes.'

He hangs up and has a satisfied look on his face- the kind he had when he broke the news that I'd been accepted by Luton FC six years ago.

'What was that about?' I ask.

'You'll see,' he says, crossing over to the fast lane, forcing the old banger to push faster.

I learned a long time ago that it is impossible to get an answer from Lewis whenever he says, *'You'll find out soon'* or *'You'll see.'* Therefore, I wait in silence for the rest of the journey.

2

CLIFF Robson has been the club's chairman for the last four years with his sizeable chunky figure and thick Scottish accent. Throughout his reign, the team always finished in the top half of the league, although failed to get promoted. Bec, his secretary, shows us into his office. As Lewis pushes me through the door, Robson is standing behind his mahogany desk. He hurries over to help with the door.

'How're you feeling, Andrew?' he says softly, as he looks down sympathetically.

'Good. The pain has lessened in the last couple of days,' I answer.

'You'll be back on the field in no time!' he says, heading back to his desk.

He places himself down, shoots Lewis a glance, and then focuses back at me.

'You are lucky to have such a special agent,' he says.

Special- different, unusual- all the same thing, I guess. 'Sure,' I answer.

'Would either of you like a drink?' he asks.

We both pass on the offer and let him continue.

'As you know, Andrew, you are one of our most valuable players. It's very unfortunate this has happened in the first game of the season. Four months is a long time to be out. I had a meeting with the manager yesterday, and he says he cannot take the risk of introducing a player to the squad who is off-form in the second half of the season. You see, we have higher hopes this year.'

I feel my heart rate speeding up and wait to see where this will lead. I dare not turn and look at Lewis, but try to concentrate and digest what Robson is saying. I feel hot and agitated (and in urgent need of a shower!) as well as my leg itching like mad beneath the plaster cast, but I try not to show any discomfort. I have never warmed to Mark Macy, the new manager, and I hope that he doesn't last the season.

'We are giving you the option of a loan, Andrew,' continues Robson. 'You can start training with them in January if you accept.'

I'm silent for a moment.

He shrugs.

Who in their right mind would want to loan a player fresh from injury? I think to myself.

'So, this is what it's about!' I say, turning to Lewis.

'You'll still be a Luton player. Plus, this will be a good opportunity for a strong comeback for next season,' explains Robson.

'And the good thing is, as far as the Football Association is concerned, you won't be on loan at all,' adds Lewis.

Robson hesitantly raises his hand, signalling for him to stay silent.

I try and make sense of what he has just said, but I can't.
'How'll that work?' I ask.

'There's a club in Northern Cyprus called Doğan,' explains
Robson. 'They aren't recognized by FIFA.'

'Actually Mr. Robson, it's pronounced Doovan,' Lewis
cuts in.

Lost for words, I stare at them both blankly. This is
entirely out of the blue and something I wasn't expecting at
all. It just shows anything can change in the world of football
in the blink of an eye.

I turn and glance at Lewis, sitting uncomfortably as if ants
are crawling up his chair. He is looking down and fidgeting
with his phone. Suddenly the room feels very claustrophobic
as if the walls are closing in. The more I think about the loan,
the more ridiculous it sounds.

'It's a beautiful place for a holiday, but why would I go
and play for a club that isn't recognized?' I ask as calmly as
possible.

Robson thinks for a moment, clears his throat, and says,
'Well, you see Andrew, no one else has shown any interest in
you because you're injured, plus subsequently Macy has
made his plans clear for this season. At the moment, the loan
seems to be the best road for you. I'm sure Mr. Orland has
already explained the problem we are having with the
accommodation too. This move was actually Mr. Orland's
idea. Doğan's president is a close friend of an old
acquaintance of his.'

For a moment, I don't talk. I keep silent and try to think straight. I can't decide whether Lewis wants my best interest, or if he's taking the easy option.

'Is this legal?' I ask.

Robson and Lewis look at each other and stall the answer to my question.

'It's the same as if you were going on holiday and kicking a ball around with a few mates down at the beach,' explains Lewis. 'There is nothing to make it illegal. As Mr. Robson noted, they are *not* recognized by FIFA.'

He always seems to have a simple answer to everything. Maybe this is the reason behind his success. I remember once he even talked a Premier League club into loaning a player who played his entire career for a third division team in Brazil, having never set foot out of the country before.

I swallow hard; take a deep breath, calming myself, 'Let me sleep on it,' I say to Robson.

'Aye,' he raises a slight smile and nods in approval.

'Let me know within two days,' he adds. 'Unfortunately, there doesn't seem to be any other option at the moment, unless you are willing to watch from the stands all season. And just one more thing, don't tell a soul. Not even family!'

When we are back in Orland's car, I question him.

'Explain,' I say bluntly. 'What was *that*?'

'Macy will ruin your career if you stay,' he replies. 'I've seen it happen before. Even if you are Pele reborn, he's so stubborn that he won't go back on his word. At least have a serious think about it, *please*.'

'So how did you pull this one out of the bag?' I ask sarcastically.

'A mate of mine from Enfield, Osman is an acquaintance of the Doğan president. We talked a couple of days ago about the football out in Northern Cyprus. It then suddenly occurred to me that as the teams out there aren't recognized by FIFA, you'll be off the radars until the end of the season. And you'll also be out of Macy's way. So basically, you'll be out the spotlight and get plenty of game time too, which should prepare you for next season! The weather is nice out there. Not like this miserable place.'

'But can they afford to loan me?'

'They offered a higher bid than the other clubs.'

'But Robson said there weren't any other clubs.'

'Exactly!'

'Good one.'

'Don't worry. Hasan Alp, Doğan's president, has more money than the actual club. He has a couple of hotels and casinos out there and a nice yacht too, I hear.'

'That's great,' I say dismissively. 'What's going on Lewis? What's with all the secrecy, and what's with all the sudden change in plan? A few months ago, we were talking about a possible move to the Premier League.'

Lewis takes a deep breath and looks away. I feel something isn't right.

'Listen,' he says eventually in almost a whisper. 'There have been some serious threats made against me. The best thing for us to do is to keep low for a while until everything settles down.'

'Threats? And what do you mean by *us?*'

'Andy, I've done something foolish. Tried to make an extra bit of cash on the side… and messed up.'

Here we go! I feel the heat creeping up my collar.

'What have you done?' I ask.

'I've gambled and lost, okay! Please don't make this more difficult than it already is!'

'Shit Lewis! I thought you gave that up long ago!'

He shrugs.

'So, … how do I come into all this?'

As he taps on the steering wheel with his thumbs, I can tell he carefully tries to construct the answer in his head first before answering.

'Got involved with some people I shouldn't have done. They want to have control over you. I was kinda tricked into it. Must have heard about the interest from the Premier League.'

Extreme anger washes over me now, yet I keep silent for the rest of the journey, and Lewis doesn't say anything either.

The Honda pulls into the accommodation's car park. These conveniently built luxury maisonettes serve a good purpose of accommodating the young footballer that hasn't yet settled down. There are about a dozen tenants, who have footballing contracts with the club and are unmarried, as well as a couple of young doctors too, and if I remember rightly a pretty young girl who is on the verge of breaking into the music business. Her producer - or lover, whoever he is, visits every so often and looks twenty years her senior. Occasionally, a few of the footballers come over to mine for drinks, but other than that, most of the tenants keep to themselves. It must be their busy lifestyles. Personally, when I come home after a busy day of training or playing a game, I want my own space - especially if it is an away game.

Jessie usually comes home late in the evening, from either a day of shopping, socialising with other WAG wannabes, or a day at the beauty salon.

I notice something that makes me feel nauseous. A silver BMW is parked at the car park, and I instantly recognize the number plate as Pablo's. Lewis's face drops as he mumbles something to himself under his breath; he's noticed it too. He parks the car close to the lifts. Pablo suddenly appears wearing a green t-shirt, torn jeans, and a black baseball cap as he swiftly strides towards his car, completely blanking us.

'It's probably not what you think,' says Lewis, giving me a cautious look.

I don't answer. It's the last thing I need, especially when I come home after surgery.

At first, I thought I was paranoid until I heard it from others. Even Lewis had warned me once. Whenever Jessie and Pablo bump into each other, whether at a party or dinner, there is extreme flirting going on and my sixth sense tells me that seeing him here is not good news.

Lewis wheels me to the door, also carrying my bag. I thank him, and he reminds me again to consider the loan to Cyprus.

Then without waiting around too long, he leaves pretty swiftly. I guess it's because he doesn't want to face the awkward situation that is about to occur. Or simply he just doesn't want to see Jessie, as he's never been fond of her from the start. Unfortunately, I have no choice but to face the music.

When I enter, she looks worn out, sweaty and red. Her freshly sprayed perfume burns my nostrils. She gives me a hug and kisses me on the lips- a kiss that doesn't taste pure - a kiss that tastes of alcohol - A kiss I don't return.

'Have you been working out?' I ask.

'I wasn't expecting you back so early,' she says.

'I bet you weren't.'

I wheel myself towards the bedroom, forcing the chair to travel as fast as possible. When I eventually get there, I see that the bed isn't made up. She follows me in, guiltily feeling the urge to explain that she was having a nap and had just awakened before I arrived. The bedroom reeks of men's B.O. as well as cheap aftershave. Although I should feel extreme anger and should be burning up inside and be sick to my stomach, I don't feel anything, just plain numbness. As cool as a cucumber, I ask her to change the sheets. She gives me a funny look but complies. After she finishes, I ask her to burn the dirty sheets.

'What do you mean, burn the sheets?' she asks, playing dumb. Or maybe she is.

'GET THE HELL OUTTA HERE!' I snap.

'GOD ANDREW! YOU PSYCHO!' she yells back, slamming the door on her way out.

Three days go by where I don't leave the house, don't answer the landline and keep my mobile turned off. I drink while feeling sorry for myself, which is probably not a great idea because of the medication- but I don't care. I keep the TV turned on the Discovery Channel, mostly watching documentaries on animals- sometimes debating whether some are more civilised than we are. Time just doesn't seem to pass. Everything is a bore, and I find myself at an all-time low. I get fed up with watching another repeat on the world's most dangerous predators, so taking a large gulp of vodka, I do something I haven't done in the last three days. Picking up the remote, I change channels. An unexpected feeling of warmth washes over me when a golden beach flashes on the screen.

'The Mediterranean is known for its golden beaches…' says the documentary while it shows a sandy beach with a bright blue sea, somewhere in southern Turkey.

I grab my mobile and press the on button. I can't seem to think straight and hesitate for a moment. I suddenly pause. I know that if I switch the phone on, it might change my life forever. Am I really prepared for this? I always felt content being institutionalised where I am.

I take a deep breath and press harder on the button. My mobile flashes and welcomes me back. Once it picks up reception, the train of messages and notifications start pouring in- each one with a racing beep- as they quickly come through. Eight of them are from Lewis. Bringing his name up from one of the missed calls, I return his call. He answers even before it rings.

'ANDREW! Are you okay? Where have you been?' he asks hurriedly.

'Yeah, I'm fine.'

'I was going to come to check on you today, Robson is-'

'I'll do it,' I cut in.

'What?'

'I accept the Cyprus deal.'

'Really? That's great! You know it makes sense.'

'How long is the beach season?'

'What? I dunno. Forget the beaches and bitches, Andrew. You need to concentrate on getting better and start training! How about Jessie?'

'It's over.'

'I'm sorry to hear that.'

'No, you're not. You never liked her anyway.'

'True. And how right I turned out to be, again!'

'So, what now?'

'I'll come and get you at three. Robson will be in his office. We need to get the paperwork started right away.

3

January 4th

IT'S been four months since the injury; finally, I'm off crutches and can even lightly jog. I've been on the verge of changing my mind about the loan to Cyprus numerous times, but none of the English clubs showed any interest, not even the ones from lower leagues. As Lewis and Robson weren't keen on a domestic loan, this made them happy.

The day fast approaches, and I find myself on a flight to Northern Cyprus via Istanbul. The plane is full and feels claustrophobic. Being their star player, and probably the only foreign one, I was expecting a business class seat- not that there is one on this flight- or at least to be somewhere closer to the front. Instead, I'm stranded in the twelfth row, next to some stocky man in a suit, who seems to be snoring although he's awake. It's been the second blow of the day. The first one was Lewis. He cancelled his flight last minute, as he's trying to complete a move for one of his players before the transfer window closes. So instead, I'm flying alone to a country that I've never been to before without a representative. Hopefully, a representative from Doğan (who I've been told speaks good English) should be greeting me at Ercan Airport.

'You travelling to Istanbul or Cyprus?' asks the man next to me, with an accent, sweat drizzling off his broad forehead.

'Cyprus,' I answer.

'Me too. I have family in *Karpaz*. They don't know I'm coming. It's a surprise for them,' he says with a big grin, wiping the sweat from his forehead with a napkin.

Politely I smile back and nod, then reach for the magazine in front.

Not getting the message 'Holiday?' he asks.

'No, work.'

'Really? What work do you do?' he keeps firing away noisily.

'I'm a footballer.'

He gives me a peculiar look like he doesn't quite believe me and says, 'Okay.'

After that, he stops with the questions, so I get a chance to close my eyes for about fifteen minutes until I feel a nudge. It's the man. He points at the air stewardess, standing over me with a tray of food. I pass the tray along to him and then gesture at the stewardess who is trying to force another tray onto me that I'll pass.

'You take it,' says the man. 'I'll eat it.'

---

[1] Karpaz: The northeast peninsula of Cyprus.

＊ ＊ ＊

After about three and a half hours, an announcement comes that we will be landing in Istanbul in twenty minutes. I'll need to hang around the airport and wait for another three hours to get a connecting flight to Northern Cyprus.

Istanbul airport is massive. The vast crowd of people pacing in all directions certainly is a culture shock compared to Luton. I wander around the duty-free shops, and then later grab a latte at one of the cafes, until eventually- after an hour delay- the boarding time finally arrives.

This plane is a lot smaller, offering unflattering warm sandwiches in plastic covers- probably heated by the plane's in-built microwave.

Eventually, we land at Ercan Airport, which is on the outskirts of Nicosia. As I walk down the steps after exiting the plane, I notice that the air isn't freezing as it is in the UK.

Ercan is a lot different compared to the chaotic atmosphere at Istanbul Airport. It's a single small building with a laid-back atmosphere and staff.

I exit arrivals, seeking the club's representative. Groups of families- young and old wait for their relatives. I notice there are a lot of children running around, which I find unusual, as back in England, I'm sure that they are usually in bed asleep this time of the evening.

'Andrew Ashford?' calls a young man wearing glasses, a black Adidas t-shirt, a grey coat, torn jeans, and bright yellow Nike trainers.

He hurries up to me, shakes my hand, and takes my suitcase, introducing himself as Ahmet from Doğan.

Now at this point, you imagine a beautiful flash limo with champagne on ice, but it can't be further from the truth.

'She is old, but gives me a good ride!' jokes Ahmet as we get into his dusty white Renault Mégane.

We drive through a lot of fields and empty spaces until we reach a small roundabout. Ahmet explains that if we go straight, we would go through Nicosia, the island's capital, which is the only divided capital city in Europe, with a United Nations buffer zone between the Turkish Cypriot and Greek Cypriot sections.

'But I don't prefer that way,' he explains as he glances right to see if any cars are approaching on the roundabout. 'We will go to Kyrenia via the mountain road.'

'How come?' I ask.

'It's faster and no traffic lights,' he explains. 'I hate those traffic lights!'

The Mégane swerves right, heading onto a secluded bit of road, towards some dark mountains that are outlined by the moonlight. Luckily the roads are driven on the left, and the cars are right-hand drives, just like the ones in the UK, therefore if I were to buy or rent a small car, I wouldn't need any time to adapt to the traffic out here.

I must admit that after both parties agreed on the loan, I spent some time researching Cyprus online, but maybe not enough, as I try to show off some of my knowledge, unsuccessfully.

'Are these the Truedos Mountains?' I ask.

'No. *The Troodos* are in the south. These are Beşparmak Dağları[2], or in English the Five Finger Mountains.'

'Oh, yes, I remember. How come they're called the Five Fingers?'

'Soon we will pass an area of the mountain where it sticks up like five fingers,' says Ahmet with an enthusiastic voice, more than willing to be a tour guide as well as the chauffeur.

It takes approximately forty minutes to reach the Colony, a colonial-style boutique hotel in the centre of the city, built with traditional yellow stone. I also notice Venetian style statues surrounding the building, giving the hotel an Italian feel, and yet the place has a hint of an Anglo feeling at the same time.

As we walk in, the sound of a piano playing jazz welcomes us. Next to the marble reception area on the left is an open bar lounge, with a grand piano at its centre, where the pianist- a man wearing a tuxedo- is thumping away nicely. To the right of the reception, there is a corridor and large golden letters that read CASINO.

'Do you gamble?' asks Ahmet, noticing me looking at it.

'I play the occasional poker,' I answer.

'Plenty of casinos here. But you have to be careful. The boss isn't too keen for the players to gamble.'

'Well, as I said, I play the occasional poker, I don't really gamble.'

---

[2] Beşparmak Dağları: Kyrenia Mountains

I think back to a couple of years ago when I had just met Jessie. We had flown to Paris for the New Year and after coming back to our hotel room from dinner and a couple of bars, drunk; she took out a deck of cards to challenge me to a game of strip poker. Although the games were never fully finished, it gave me plenty of practice.

'Andrew Ashford!' Ahmet says to the receptionist. '*Rezervasyon Hasan bey tarafından yaptılmıştır*[3].'

'Welcome to the Colony, Mr. Ashford. Please can I have your passport while you fill in this form,' says the man behind the reception desk with relatively good English.

I get my key and Ahmet rushes off, after completing his mission for the evening. He will be back at nine in the morning to escort me to the club building so that the contract for the loan can be signed.

The room is cosy with a small double bed, and a good view of a nicely lit up nearby castle, which appears the same golden colour as the hotel. I throw myself on the bed and open my suitcase. Lewis informed me that after the contract is signed, I would move to a residence close to the training ground and stadium.

Despite Lewis occasionally getting my hopes up for a Premier League move, I admit that I am no top-level footballer. After the age of twenty-eight, hoping to play for a Premier League or any top European club would be a long shot. Still, I didn't expect some schoolboy to pick me up from the airport

---

[3] Rezervasyon Hasan bey tarafından yaptılmıştır: Mr. Hasan has made the reservation. (In Turkish)

with his dad's old banger. Not that I was expecting a limo either. What I was hoping for was maybe some kind of briefing from one of the club's officials.

My phone buzzes with Lewis's name flashing on the screen. I answer.

'Andrew! How was the flight? Did you get to the hotel?'

'Yeah, I did. Everything is okay… I think.'

'That's great! What did they say?'

'Well, a boy who looked about twelve picked me up from the airport. He said that the contract would be signed tomorrow morning.'

'Brilliant! I will give you another call tomorrow around noon then. What's the time out there now?'

'Twenty-two twenty,' I answer.

'Right, so you are two hours ahead. Anyway, gotta dash,' he says hanging up.

Typical Lewis- not even a goodbye.

I leave the room with a sudden onset of hunger, seeking a quick bite to eat. A small advertising screen flashes inside the lift, displaying Misty's Roof Bar, situated at the roof of the hotel. Pressing the level-five button, I go up to check it out. The roof is covered with a large tent, with an outdoor swimming pool on the other side. A guitarist with long hair sits on a tall stool thumping away on a Spanish guitar, with a young lady seated next to him holding a microphone, singing *Lady in Red*.

I sit at one of the small round tables. The lights around the sides project purple, giving the place a romantic but mysterious feel. As it's Sunday, the place isn't too full. An English looking couple is seated on a table near the stage gulping down bottles of local beer and at the other end, six local girls in their early to mid-twenties are having small cups of tea or coffee. The cups seem incredibly small, so I assume that they are drinking espressos, but oddly one of the girls seems to be telling a story to the others of some kind while bringing the cup right up to her face and looking deep inside. The others concentrate hard on what she has to say, occasionally laughing and commenting.

I get so transfixed in their world of small cups that I barely notice the waiter standing next to me, trying to hand over a drinks menu. I thank him and ask for the food menu instead. He says he can only serve snacks at this time of evening and tells me the options. I order a club sandwich and a small bottle of sparkling water, which, to my delight, arrive pretty swiftly. Enjoying every bite of the club sandwich with fries on the side, I gulp it all down in no more than ten minutes, then scan around to ask for the bill, but when I can't see the waiter, I decide to go up to the bar and pay there instead. One of the girls from the table of the small cups is also waiting. She looks at me with her large green eyes and smiles.

'Looks like they don't want our money tonight,' she jokes.

I get caught off guard by her good English.

'Yes, maybe we should just walk out,' I say.

She giggles.

'By the way, what was in those small cups on your table. Are there stories written inside them or something?'

'Yes, something like that. You must be new here.'

'I just arrived an hour ago. It's *that* obvious, huh?'

'Erm, yes! They are Turkish coffees. After finishing, the fortune is read from the bottom of the cup.'

'I see…'

'Here he is,' she says, as the waiter- disappointingly-walks up to us.

She pays, smiles, and says goodnight. I can't take my eyes off of her as she walks back to her friends. She looks stunning, absolutely stunning in her tight leather trousers and a black jacket. I've never had a thing for ponytails, but she's definitely an exception.

I head back to my room for an early night, ahead of the big day tomorrow, and eventually doze off while thinking about *her*, the mysterious girl whose name I don't even know.

4

January 5th

IN the early hours of the morning, I hear someone outside singing acapella. It suddenly occurs to me that it's the call for prayer coming from a nearby mosque. After that, I can't go back to sleep - I keep thinking about the day ahead, and then suddenly, I get distracted by a beautiful young lady walking into my thoughts, the one I had spoken to up at Misty's. I doubt I'll ever see her again, which somehow saddens me. I feel a fool feeling this way, as I don't even know her. Before I know it, it's twenty minutes past eight. Brushing my teeth, I look at my sleepy reflection. Large bags hang from the bottom of my swollen eyes and my face seems incredibly pale. The stubble makes me look tired and older then I am. I think after four days without shaving, today would be a good time to start.

After showering and freshening up, I choose what to wear from my limited collection of clothes for today's occasion. I then take the lift down to the restaurant for breakfast and happy to see a rich selection of cereal varieties.

Helping myself to a generous portion of muesli and fruit, I get a big spoonful of honey and feed it around the mountain of muesli. Subtly I scan the other tables, hoping that *she* might be there, but of course, she isn't, as these types of coincidences only happen in movies.

Just as I'm scraping the bottom of the bowl, my phone rings, a local-number flashing on the screen.

I answer.

'Good morning Andrew! Are you ready?' comes Ahmet's voice through the phone speaker.

He sounds happier and even more energetic then he did last night.

'Morning Ahmet. Yes, I just finished my breakfast,' I tell him.

I find Ahmet at reception flirting with one of the receptionists. I could hear his exaggerated laugh echoing from the other end of the corridor.

'Andrew!' he calls out, shaking my hand. 'Are you ready to go!'

Ready to go I am- but to sign a loan for a club that isn't FIFA registered, which I've never heard of before will be either the bravest or the dumbest thing I've ever done in my entire life, I think to myself as I follow him out of the front entrance and across the road.

'Where'd you park?' I ask when I notice that we are walking towards the town.

'No need to drive,' he says. 'The club is just behind that building over there.'

For January, it's relatively warm with a clear sky. I remove my leather jacket and observe the surroundings of this small harbour city. Most of the buildings are old, with newer developments sprouting out between them- some giving Kyrenia a boost of glamour, while others are looking slightly out of place. I feel the warmth here, a hospitable feeling that I rarely experienced before. I cast my concentration back to what Ahmet is saying as he happily talks away without stopping, giving me a brief history lesson, the type that you'd expect to hear from a tour guide.

'That is Kyrenia Castle. The Venetians originally built it,' he explains, pointing at the large castle next to the sea. 'Inside is a museum. There's an ancient shipwreck!'

'Sounds fascinating. I'll have to put that down on my list of things to do,' I say and mean it.

After a five-minute walk through the city square, we arrive at a very narrow road with a building I guess is as old as the castle itself. A tall minaret, built from yellow stone, overlooks the harbour. We come to a building with a wooden flagpole sticking out from one of the top windows, with the club's navy-blue and yellow flag waving from it.

'Welcome to the Dogan Türk Birliği club building!' Ahmet says with pride.

'It's quite an ancient building.'

'Yes. Originally it was built as part of the harbour. Most buildings in this part of town are ancient.'

We walk up a narrow staircase that has marble steps with wooden railings and into a room surrounded with sofas that have seen better days. A small T.V. is sitting on a little wooden table at the far end, airing some sports programme in Turkish. It can easily be someone's living room; I keep thinking to myself. Hundreds of framed pictures hang covering the walls.

Most are historic pre-season and pre-match photos, all dated, as well as a photo of a single player or two.

Three men sit sipping Turkish coffees and talk amongst themselves, ignoring the T.V. One is wearing a grey t-shirt and jeans, with a camera hanging from his neck. The other is sporting a light blue tracksuit with the club's logo on, and the third man is in a smart navy suit and has greying hair.

'*Günaydın*[4],' Ahmet says to them.

'Good morning!' answers the one wearing the suit in English, and enthusiastically gets up to shake my hand. 'Good to meet you, Andrew. I am Hasan Alp, the club's president.'

So, at last, I get to meet *The* Hasan Alp. He asks me if I had a good flight and if I am happy with the hotel room. I thank him. He introduces me to the man in the tracksuit, a heavily built man with a gut, who obviously likes his food and drink.

'This is Remzi Alkan. He is our head coach,' he says proudly.

Not saying much, Remzi shakes my hand with a firm grip, examining me from head to toe.

'What would you like to drink?' asks Alp. 'A coffee perhaps?' he adds in an almost perfect English accent.

'Yes, in fact, I wouldn't mind trying a Turkish coffee,' I say.

'Looks like you already fit in,' he says with a smile. 'How would you like it?'

'In one of those small cups that you have yours in,' I say.

Both men laugh. Remzi mumbles something to Alp in Turkish, looking amused by my comment.

---

[4] Günaydın: Good Morning

'No, what I mean is would you like it sade... meaning plain, orta... as in medium sweet or şekerli, which means sweet?'

Contemplating it for a moment, I ask for medium, thinking that it will be the safest option.

Alp explains that soon an official from the Cyprus Turkish Football Association will arrive with some documents so that the loan procedures can get started.

The Turkish coffee comes right away with a small glass of water on the side. It reminds me of an overly thick sweet espresso. After about the fifth sip, I start to enjoy it. When I finish, the official still hasn't turned up.

'So, do I turn it upside down now for the reading?' I ask, looking at the thick mud of coffee at the bottom of the cup.

They laugh again.

'That's more what the ladies to do,' explains Alp.

'Unless you want to read our fortunes,' chuckles Remzi with a strong Cypriot accent.

I look at the time and realize we've been waiting for over an hour.

'Shall we give him a call?' I say.

'Don't worry, he'll be here,' Alp assures me with a smile. 'This is Cyprus. Everything is slow. You'll gradually get used to it.'

I remove my phone from my pocket to check for any messages. That's when I realize, I have a missed call from Lewis, so I call him back.

'Andy!' he answers. 'Have you signed yet?'

'No, not yet,' I say.

'Listen. If anyone Russian approaches you and asks you to sign anything, say you're not interested. Just walk away.'

'Why? Has anyone clocked on to the fact that I'm here?' I whisper, moving away from the coach and club president, with my hand covering the mouthpiece.

'Not at all, but no harm in being too cautious.'

'Great! Once again, I'd like to thank you very much for putting me into this situation.'

'Don't worry, Andy. Everything is going to be all right! Anyway, must fly.'

Almost forty minutes later, a tall man in a suit and tie turns up with the loan documents. He doesn't seem apologetic about being late and walks straight into the conference room next door.

After a few signatures that make me a valid Doğan player on loan from Luton FC, and then a couple of unnecessary poses for the media, again I find myself in Ahmet's old banger, heading towards the hospital for a medical examination. We arrive at a small clinic somewhere in the side streets of Kyrenia, which for some reason, in no way drums confidence into me. Doing a blood test- I understand, but the chest x-ray is beyond me. Why the unnecessary radiation?

A young girl with a ponytail forces me up against a board- tells me to keep still and to hold my breath- while she pushes the button.

'Your licence should be ready by Wednesday,' says Ahmet, as we exit the hospital after the examination. 'Then you can start training.'

'And when's the next game again?' I ask.

'In two weeks against Mağusa Türk Gücü.'

'Home or away?'

'Away at Famagusta.'

I try and think back to my map and the search I did online.

'That's the city in the east, right?' I ask proudly.

'Right,' he confirms with a smile.

We drive past a muddy field where about six or seven young boys are kicking a ball around.

'Is football the main sport here?'

Ahmet smiles and replies, 'Basketball is very popular too. I prefer it.'

'So, what's our coach like?'

'Remzi? He's grumpy mostly, but he's okay. He likes to play attacking football. If the team concedes a goal, he expects them to score three. Just don't be surprised if he shouts and throws things around the changing room at half time,' laughs Ahmet.

'Nothing I'm not used to,' I say.

Just as I step into my hotel room, Lewis calls.

'Congratulations mate!' he says with a chirpy voice.

I let out a half-hearted, 'Cheers.'

'Listen,' he says. 'My phone will be off for a couple of days. If anyone asks where I am, just say you haven't heard from me.'

Here we go!

'Jesus Lewis! Now you want me to lie for you?'

'It's not a lie, though, is it?'

I don't reply.

'It will all pass... I promise!'

'*Pass?* I've been sent away to another country! No one has been officially informed! And I still don't understand how I'm involved in your gambling addictions!'

'Okay, listen,' he says with a slightly shaky voice. 'Are you alone?

'Yes, I am.'

'Right, you know these men I owe money to?'

'Go on.'

'I was way over my limit... so I ended up gambling you too.'

There's a moment's silence, as I try and digest the information.

'What do you mean by *gambled me too*?'

He clears his throat and replies, 'Well, they wouldn't even accept the car. They made it very clear that they wanted your agency rights.'

Again, I am silent and calmly try and make sense of the whole thing.

'What do you mean?' I ask.

'They want to have control over you, Andy. They want all my commission. They must have heard about the interest from the Premier League.'

'So, you gambled me?'

'Well, not directly. They took my wallet, so I don't do a runner.'

'You gave them your wallet?'

'Course not! Luckily, I was smart enough to go there with my spare wallet with just the cash for gambling and some outdated credit cards and an expired driver's licence.'

'That's crazy!'

'Isn't it? But it's only a matter of time for them to clock on, which is why I need to be low key for a while.'

'Listen, Lewis, I know how much you've done for me in the past, and I appreciate it, but this time you've crossed the line!'

'I know Andy, and I'm sorry. They didn't leave me much choice. I promise I'll make it up to you! But listen, these men are dangerous. They forced me into it! That's how dangerous they are!'

'So what would you do if I didn't get injured? Wait a minute… my injury wasn't a coincidence. Was it?'

'I told you, Andy. They're dangerous.'

'Why don't we call the police. We know who injured me! We can try and get a name.'

'No! We can't do that! No police! We have no proof that you'd been injured on purpose!'

'Why not? Why no police?'

'Because I'll get my agency licence removed. FIFA will crucify me! And publicity like that could spell the end of what's left of your career too.'

He's right. Lewis has been my agent since day one, and publicity involving corruption would harm my career. My face heats up with anger, my heart races faster, and I feel breathless as if I'm being strangled.

'You can go to hell!' I snap at him.

'I'll contact you soon,' he says in a calm voice. 'Good luck with your first training session.'

5

January 7th

NEWS came in about an hour ago that my medical is approved- making me a certified Doğan player- therefore granting me access to play in the North Cyprus Super League. As most of the players in the league are either amateurs or semi-professionals. They all have their day jobs. Training typically starts at 5:30 pm, as opposed to the professional team's early morning sessions that I'm used to.

The training sessions take place at two different grounds. The one opposite the Pia Bella Hotel is a full-sized football pitch that is well looked after. Unfortunately, today we are at the other, located close to the city centre next to the 20 Temmuz Stadium. It has an uneven ground that slightly slopes to one side and smaller than the other. I can't help think that it's a perfect recipe for ankle injuries.

Alkan stands by the sideline with a baseball cap and his whistle hanging around his neck. After getting us to do stretches, he orders a run around the field ten times, before calling us back to the centre circle.

'It's important to be match fit! So, plenty of cardio! I want cardio!' he repeats.

After some passing practice, we get separated into two groups and finally play a game amongst ourselves.

It's not long until my team is attacking from the left-wing. A short skinny fella, whose name I don't yet know, dribbles past a defender. I get into a good position ready to pull the trigger as soon the pass comes in, but to my despair, something happens that baffles me. It's something I haven't experienced during my professional career before; the winger takes a long shot instead of passing. It's such an awful attempt that it lobs metres away from the goal with the ball hanging in the air like some rugby conversion. I turn and look at the coach waiting for him to criticise, but instead, he claps and shouts *'Good try!'*

Clenching my teeth, I keep quiet and continue.

Two minutes later, another opportunity presents itself. Although I am through on goal, the midfielder passes the ball back.

'Oh, come on! I was through!' I cry with irritation.

After twenty minutes, the game is over, and I'd barely touched the ball.

'Coach! What's wrong with these people!? No one's passing!'

'That's normal,' Alkan says dismissively. 'They don't know you well enough yet.'

'That's charming,' I sigh, surprised by his laidback attitude.

Some memories come rushing back to my school days when everyone thought they were the next Ronaldinho. There was less passing and more long-distance shooting.

Ahmet waits by the gate, lost in his phone. At first, he doesn't notice me, and when he does, he greets me half-heartedly.

'How was it?' he asks, still looking at his phone as we slowly start walking to the car.

'Not great. How am I supposed to score if no one bloody passes.'

'Yes, I've noticed. But relax. They will, once they get to know you,' he explains, opening the car door.

He drives me to the hotel to get my belongings and then to the flat. The living room overlooks the sea and both the bedrooms have a generous view of the Kyrenia Mountains. The club is renting the flat to some of the players.

As I'm unpacking, the doorbell rings. A man stands at the door wearing a grin.

'Hello,' he says, putting out his hand. 'I'm Peter Promise. We're neighbours and also teammates. I live one floor down.'

'Good to meet you. Andrew Ashford,' I introduce myself, shaking his hand and inviting him in. 'Yes, I recognized you from training. Sorry, as I just moved in, I have nothing to offer but water.'

'Don't sweat it. I can recommend a couple of good markets nearby,' he answers. 'One is just a five-minute walk from here.'

'Thanks, I'm sure I'll get used to finding my way around.'

'You coming here is a big surprise. An interesting decision,' he says, fishing for an answer.

'It's an unpredictable world,' is the best I can come up with without giving too much away.

'So how did you end up here, Peter? What's your story?' I ask, turning the tables on him.

'It's my second year at the club. I came as a student. I study economics at the American University of Kyrenia.'

'So, you are semi-professional.'

'Well, I used to play for a team in Nigeria. But my father pushed me to come to university here. A friend recommended me for the trials, and luckily I got in.'

'It seems pretty quiet out here. Not much to do.'

He gives me an odd look. 'Are you joking? This is the casino capital of the Mediterranean! Some nice discos and bars around too.'

'I thought the club didn't approve of us going to the casinos.'

'No one really checks or cares what you do. As long as you perform well on the pitch.'

'Well, maybe you can be my tour guide,' I say with a smile.

'Actually, one of the players is holding a small party at his villa in Bellapais tonight. I'll be going around eight if you are interested. They are doing the Cypriot style barbeque thing.'

'Sure, if they don't mind me gate-crashing.'

'Not at all. It's an open invitation for all players.'

Although the last couple of days have worn me out, this is precisely the type of introduction I need to get to know my new teammates.

'Sounds good,' I say.

※ ※ ※

We drive up to Bellapais in his silver Ford Fiesta. Bellapais is a small village up in the mountains about five miles from Kyrenia. The picturesque view just before entering the town takes me by surprise. An ancient building shines, reflecting its golden lights in the distance and hovering alone in the darkness of the night.

'What's that?' I ask.

'The Abbey,' Peter answers. 'Beautiful, isn't it?'

Intrigued by the beauty of Bellapais Abbey, I later read up on the ancient landmark. Monks who were fleeing Palestine after the fall of Jerusalem to Selahaddin Eyyubi⁵ originally built the French Gothic abbey in the 13th century. To this day most of it remains in good condition and attracts a high number of tourists from around the world.

It takes about fifteen minutes to reach the villa, which is high up in the mountains. An artificial waterfall runs down behind the outer stairs and into the Olympic sized pool on the ground floor. I can almost smell the champagne as we drive up and park opposite the golden gates.

A loud bass thumps away from inside, with loud talking and laughter, as we walk up.

---

⁵ Selahaddin Eyyubi was the first sultan of Egypt and Syria and the founder of the Ayyubid dynasty (1137 – 4 March 1193)

'Hackers is at it again,' says Peter.

'Hackers?'

'Hakan, the left-winger… Hackers. Poor guy… always a sub. But I'm sure he doesn't mind. After a few drinks, he starts to DJ at every bloody party. The man's got no rhythm and can't even mix, but no one will tell him that to his face!'

We approach the door that's been left ajar and invite ourselves inside.

I recognize most of the players from the afternoon training session as I follow Peter through the crowded corridor. The music is awful with an English and Turkish song competing to catch up with each other's beat.

We then enter a large room, which must have at least fifty people inside. A giant marble table rests against the wall with bottles of Efes beer on one side, two bottles of champagne on the other, and a bottle of Black Label whisky in the centre. Next to the drinks table is a sliding door that leads to a wide terrace, with stairs that go down to the pool. The smell from the barbeque takes over the entire room. Peter helps himself to a whisky and coke, while I grab a bottle of Efes beer. We get offered large pita bread with a generous helping of shish kebabs, grilled *hellim*, and tomatoes all crammed inside. The old boy with the short white hair, scruffy moustache, and a large belly is in charge of the grill out in the terrace and tries to force another mixed pitta into my hand, but I kindly reject his offer. However, Peter doesn't and is already halfway through the first one.

---

[6] Hellim: Cypriot Cheese

43

We lose each other in the crowd, and I'm left chatting to two of the other players who introduce themselves as Adil and Oktay. Oktay is the host and says he's happy that I came along. Two young ladies are standing next to them, Hülya and Serpil, who are either their wives or girlfriends.

'I'd love to play football in England,' says Oktay. 'Coming here is like taking a step back.'

'I went to college in London,' cuts in Adil. 'Played quite a bit of Sunday league.'

After chatting for a while, I start getting overheated when Adil asks me why I preferred Doğan over Luton. I excuse myself and make my way past the drinks table and out the sliding doors for some fresh air.

It's a crisp winter's night, with no clouds shadowing the sky, and the moonlight shining bright. A few people scattered around the terrace enjoy the barbeque.

From the corner of my eye, I notice someone staring at me. I turn and get a quick glimpse. A man who seems to be in his forties, with short blonde hair and frowning grey eyes, is watching me. My heart skips a beat when I remember what Lewis said about keeping clear of anyone Russian.

I take a few steps further towards the stairs that lead down to the pool. I look at the reflection through the glass on my left and notice the man is not there anymore. Not trusting the refection, I turn to look - he has gone. I sigh a deep sigh and head towards the end of the porch.

Down by the pool, I hear a girl's voice. Although I cannot understand what she's saying, I can tell by her tone that she's arguing on the phone. I get closer and slowly start making my way down until I reach the bottom. When she's in full view, I am stunned to see that it's the girl from Misty's Bar. I wait for her to hang up.

Taking a deep breath in, 'Good evening.' I say.

She turns, and I notice she's been crying, but she subtly wipes her tears with her palms when she sees me. From her expression, it's evident that she recognizes me straight away- almost like she's been expecting me.

'Well, if it isn't the new star of the team,' she says with her face lighting up.

Jokingly, I take a quick look around in confusion.

'I wouldn't go that far,' I answer.

'You're turning this into a habit,' she says.

'What's that?'

'Creeping up behind me at night.'

'Purely coincidental.'

'Relax, I'm only messing with you,' she giggles. 'Cyprus isn't that big. You tend to bump into the same people. Especially here in Kyrenia.'

'You look upset,' I say.

She falls silent. I can tell she wants to tell me something but decides against it.

'It's nothing important,' she eventually says.

'It must be if you've been crying.'

'It's a long story. I don't want to bore you with it,' she says, staring into the pool.

'I have all the time in the world.'

She looks deep into my eyes and smiles- a look that gets my heart beating faster- a feeling I haven't felt in a very long time.

'There's someone I'm-'

'YO, ANDREW! YOU COMIN' UP?' a voice calls from the terrace.

It's Peter. I smile, trying not to show my frustration at the moment being ruined.

'Well, apparently you haven't got all the time in the world,' she smiles.

'ANDREW MAN!?'

'COMING RIGHT UP PETER!'

I turn and look back at her. "What's your name?" I ask.

'Aysha,' she replies.

'Pleased to meet you,' I say, bringing out my hand to shake hers.

'And according to the media, you're Andrew Ashford, the new star signing from Luton.'

'Not sure about the latter part,' I laugh.

We don't let go for a long moment, as she warms her cold hand in mine.

I then head back up and follow Peter back to his car.

On the way back, he is silent. I get a feeling that he wants to share something, but can't bring himself to say it. I don't say anything either. I don't know him well enough to ask. At the moment, the only thing on my mind is Aysha. After about five minutes, I break the silence.

'It's beautiful here. Very relaxed,' I say.

'Everyone says the same thing,' replies Peter. 'Especially when they first come.'

'I get the feeling that you are not completely content.'

He turns and looks at me, 'You are right. I'm not.'

'How come?' I ask.

'I miss my wife,' he answers. 'She's in Nigeria.'

'Can't she come over?'

'That's my plan. To get her into one of the universities here next year.'

For the rest of the drive home, I hear Peter's love story of how he met his wife and how he proposed to her, but both families had disapproved of the marriage because of the class and religious differences. Somehow, he ended up studying here without her.

'Just a friendly bit of advice, keep away from her.' he says as he pulls up outside the apartment block.

'What do you mean?' I ask.

'Aysha. Keep away from her.'

'What do you mean?' I ask.

'Man, are you crazy!? She's only the club president's daughter!'

'She's Alp's daughter?'

'Yes!'

'We were just talking, nothing happened.'

'Yeah, but I saw the way you two were looking at each other. I just don't want you to get hurt, and anyway, she's already engaged to someone!'

'I see,' I say, disappointed.

'He's some medical student named Umut. His family is friends with the Alps.'

The night ends with a kick in the teeth. It looks like Aysha is off-limits.

6

AFTER three weeks of training, I feel my old form slowly creeping back, although at times, a sharp pain kindly reminds me of the past injury, warning me to take things easy.

The climate in Cyprus has undoubtedly been a pleasant surprise. It's match day, the first game of the New Year and while most of Europe is under snow with a long list of weekend games postponed, here in Cyprus, the sun shines bright with hardly a cloud in sight. What a way to start the year!

Although, I played against big clubs before, but still get out of bed feeling nervous and nauseous, as the pressure of being a lone striker plays in the back of my mind. The club seems to be entirely dependent on me, something that I have never experienced when playing in England- maybe in my schooldays - but at the moment that certainly isn't a salient point and so the nerves aren't helped by the fact that I'm the key man.

Mağusa Türk Gücü are tenth in the league, two places and three points above us. They finished the first half of the season in good spirits, winning the last five games. A win would see us move above them on goal difference.

Getting breakfast out the way with a quick piece of toast and a cup of Nescafe, I jump into the newly rented Polo, and make my way to the club building. The team talk is a fascinating one, with the coach thumping his marker against the whiteboard and yelling stuff in Turkish. Luckily Ahmet is there to translate for the English-speaking players, which happens to be just Peter and me.

'Help each other! You must always help each other. Make ball do work. And use wings! Many many times use wings…' repeats Ahmet, trying to sound as important as the coach.

After Alkan's team-talk, followed by a few inspirational words from Adil, the captain, we make our way into the next room for an early lunch. On the menu is thick pasta with boiled chicken, topped with a grated hellim cheese and dried mint. This dish, which is one of the specialties in Cyprus, is known as *makarına bulli*. It tastes so good that I can easily eat another plate, but the portions are kept to a minimum and just enough for an energy boost for the game. After lunch, Turkish coffees are served.

We eventually board the yellow and navy-blue team bus, with massive team logos covering both sides. Famagusta is approximately forty miles away from Kyrenia. It takes a good hour to reach. Known for its mediaeval architecture such as the Salamis ruins and its ancient city wall, the city also boasts the deepest harbour in the entire island.

After a quiet, but bumpy hour, the bus finds a secluded spot outside the Dr. Fazıl Küçük Stadium, where the city's team,

Mağusa Türk Gücü play their home games. The stands are on one side of the stadium and a wall on the other- just like 20 Temmuz Stadı, where we play our home games. Their home support outnumbers ours, occupying around eighty percent of the stands.

Disaster strikes right from the start after we lose the ball in midfield. One chip to their tall centre-forward and he coolly places it to the right-hand side of our keeper. The sound is almost deafening with loud cheers and beeping of horns.

'Come on! Heads up' cries Adil, the captain, clapping his hands, trying his best to keep the motivation from fading.

After the goal, our opponents switch to a more defensive mode keeping us at arm's length. Apart from a few long shots, our game is lame. We go into the changing room with our heads hanging low for a half time grilling from Remzi.

Whether it's the grilling that works or Mağusa Türk Gücü's loss of energy, things change fifteen minutes into the second half, as our right-winger, Sabri paces down the wing, dribbling past two midfielders and then crossing high from near the corner flag. I wait in front of goal, focusing hard on the high ball, before making a diagonal run to get to it before the opposition's keeper, who is a six-foot-something giant, with a belly on him. A shove from behind and a shoulder barge doesn't stop me from making contact with the ball, as I head it down towards the ground out of the keeper's reach. The ball bounces off the ground and into the back of the net. Our fans cheer and start chanting my name as my teammates swarm around me. At last, I finally start feeling like a genuine part of the team. The final score finishes with a 3-1 win to Doğan Türk

51

Birliği, with me scoring my first hat trick in my first ever game for them.

At the end of the game, Remzi walks straight up to me, wraps his arms around my shoulders and kisses me on both cheeks.

'Amazing!' he cries, with a big grin, exposing his large gapped teeth. 'That was amazing!'

With pride, I enter the changing rooms- if they can pass as that. The cramped grey room, where a stale smell of urine lingers, has never once seen paint on its walls- with benches and rusty hooks running along the sides, stubbornly keeping most of the sunlight out. A basin awkwardly sticks out of the wall at the far end, with a small faded mirror asymmetrically hanging above it. There is a cubicle at the other end with a toilet inside. When I say toilet, I mean a hole in the ground. That's the way the old traditional ones were. As for the shower… that has to wait until I return to my flat in Kyrenia.

I'll certainly never forget the journey back. I'm not talking about the strong smell of body odour, but the team chanting something in Turkish, with my name included. I have no idea what they are saying, but I cannot help but laugh. Peter, who is sitting next to me is also in tears of laughter and gives me a high-five, 'Good work, bro!'

It's been a while since I've been named *man of the match*.

When we finally arrive at the club's car park in Kyrenia, Ahmet is congratulating the team.

'Good start!' he says to me with a proud look. 'We expect the same every game.'

'Not sure I can promise that, but I can certainly try,' I answer with a smile.

'I've booked a table at the meyhane for tonight!' he says.

'The what?'

'I'll come and pick you and Peter up at eight. Make sure you have an empty stomach.'

Later on that evening, we arrive at the meyhane. When I see the quantity of food, that's when I understand what he meant by having an empty stomach.

Meyhanes have always been part of the eastern European culture, and extremely popular in Northern Cyprus. The origin of the word Meyhane comes from Persian, with a combination of two words. *Mey* (wine) and *khāneh* (house).

On the skirt of the mountain- between Zeytinlik and Lapta- lies hidden the meyhane, simply named *The Meyhane*. Upon entering, we are welcomed with loud traditional acoustic music, from a three-person band, as they walk from table to table performing songs requested by the joyous customers.

We join a long table near the fireplace, where the Doğan players indulge in the large variety of mezes, generously scattered all over the table. Without getting asked, I get poured a rakı- the preferred drink- made from aniseed and grapes.

While the waiter serves grilled *hellim* and *köfte*, that's when I sense him at the other end of the crowded room- with his grey eyes cold like a shark's, not quite observing me, as that would be too obvious. Indeed, he is the same man that was at the house party at Bellapais. On his table are two other men. Who are these people? Are they here to spy on me? Or is it just my paranoia? Lewis' words echo in my head '*If anyone Russian approaches you and asks you to sign anything, just walk away.*'

Then they mysteriously disappear during the night, getting lost in the drunken meyhane crowd. The rakı goes straight to my head, helping me relax, leaving its strong aniseed taste in my mouth. Over all it's been a tiring, but a good day. As for the meyhane culture, I can certainly get used to this lifestyle.

7

March 2ⁿᵈ

THE following games end with two home wins and a draw. Although I only score one goal in the second home game, the coach is relatively happy with my performance. To be fair, I did set up three.

The next stop that evening is Lord's Palace Casino, thinking that a couple of blackjack games won't do any harm. Usually, I get called or invited to the team's social weekend activities, but this week no one has mentioned anything. That's because Ahmet is away in Istanbul for a couple of days for the derby game between Fenerbahçe and Galatasaray.

Getting five hundred Liras worth of chips, I choose a table that's not overly crowded. A bald man with glasses is seated next to me and politely nods and smiles as I join the table. Next to him is an Arabic looking man with a neatly shaved beard who seems overdressed with a dinner jacket and a bow tie. He has no expression on his face and appears to be ignoring everything around him. A lady with dark red hair joins us and sits herself down opposite me. For a quick second, she glances over and smiles. The dealer swiftly shuffles and starts dealing the cards out.

Unfortunately, the blackjack game does not end as well as the football match, and I end up losing five hundred Liras within twenty minutes.

I excuse myself from the table and make my way towards the exit.

'Better luck next time,' says a voice from behind.

The lady with the dark red hair passes, heading towards the bar with a handful of chips in her hand.

'Thank you,' I say. 'I seem to be out of practice.'

'It's more luck than practice,' she says. 'Bit like life sometimes.'

'Yes, I suppose it is.'

We end up at the bar.

'Do you mind?' I ask, pointing to the empty barstool, next to where she's sitting.

'No, go ahead,' she says with a harsh domineering accent, which I guess is Eastern European.

I take a seat.

'What are you drinking?'

'Brandy sour,' she replies.

'Two brandy sours, please,' I call to the barman.

She puffs on an electronic cigarette and lustfully stares at me - a stare I am not sure I quite welcome, as to be honest, I still can't get Aysha out of my mind. And that's when I realize that I've never fallen this deep for anyone before.

'You come here often?' I ask.

'Occasionally. You?'

'This is my first time in a casino in Cyprus.'

'Really?' she says, taking a sip of the brandy sour.

I also take a sip, welcoming the sweet taste of the coating of sugar decorating the rim of the glass.

'I'm Andrew,' I introduce myself.

'Zoya,' she says.

I still have no idea where this will lead. I know every country has its own rules about this sort of thing, but I give it the benefit of the doubt and go with the flow, although something doesn't seem quite right- more than a little pretentious.

'So, what do you do?' I ask.

'A couple of things. Mostly translations.'

'All right.'

I wait a moment for her to ask me what I do, but she never does. Instead, she quietly observes her cocktail while running her index finger down the cold glass.

'Where are you from?' I ask.

'I'm half Russian, half French,' she answers. 'I'm guessing you're from England?'

'Yes,' I reply.

'Holiday?'

'I'm a footballer.'

'Really? But not professional, surely.'

I sigh, 'Course I am. What makes you think I'm not?'

She giggles and answers, 'I know the teams here are, let's say, not so professional. I mean, come on. The country isn't even recognized.'

Her phone buzzes. It's a message. She swiftly replies and then chucks the phone into her bag.

'Thanks for the drink,' she says.

'You're welcome. First time I ever tried it.'

'Really? It's the most popular cocktail in Cyprus.'

'Refreshing,' I say. 'Very light too.'

'They use local brandy and lemons.'

She looks into my eyes and smiles. Leaning forward, she strokes my arm and asks, 'So, you fancy a walk?'

Why not? I think to myself. As stunning as she is, there is something *out of place* about her. Something I can't quite put my finger on, but I've been here for almost a month now, and I need to meet new people outside the circle of the team. Maybe now is a good time to start. Little do I know that after tonight I will never be seeing Zoya again.

We get our coats from the cloakroom and walk out into the dark street. The sound of the waves echoes from the harbour as we head away from the hotel.

Kyrenia has two harbours, not too far from each other. One is the old touristic, which is overshadowed by the castle. The newer is just down the road from the Lord's Palace Hotel. It is here where ferries go back and forth to Turkey. And it is from this direction a black BMW with tinted windows comes to a screeching stop next to us.

'*Sorry*,' Zoya softly whispers into my ear.

A man gets out from the passenger's side and opens the rear door for me to get in. Another man sits on the other side behind the driver. He has white hair and a distinctive scar across his face, kind of reminding me of an older version of Tony Montana.

'Mr. Ashford, come in. Let's talk.' he says.

He has a distinctive Eastern European accent. I turn to run, but the man outside is built like a brick house and is standing right behind me. I get into the car.

The man inside, with white hair, looks up at Zoya and says, 'Thank you my darling.'

She nods, avoiding all eye contact, and walks away back towards the hotel.

The bitch set me up! I think to myself. *I sat having a cocktail with her while all this time we were waiting for this man to come.*

'A charmer, isn't she?' he says. 'Thank you for being so patient while waiting.'

'What do you want?' I ask.

'Now that's the kind of attitude I'm looking for... What do *I* want?'

The car heads off towards the main road.

'Where are you taking me?'

'We'll have a little drive around as we talk,' he says, taking out some documents from a thin black folder resting next to him. 'It's comical. It's the dream of every local player here to play at a higher level. Even to play for lower league clubs in Europe is their dream. As long as they are FIFA listed. I'm not talking about the Premier League. No, that's just too grand. And here you are rotting away, committing career suicide.'

'What do you want?' I repeat.

'I wish Lewis was here to see this moment. It's been fun this little game of hide and seek.'

'I'm not signing anything!'

'Even if it's for a mid-table Premier League team with high expectations this year? I am talking of a possible European cup place for next season.'

As tempting as the offer sounds, Lewis had warned me that these guys are dirt- which is pretty much a given by the way they approached me.

'I already have an agent,' I answer.

The man grins patronisingly. A grin that makes me feel on edge.

'I see you also like to gamble, Mr. Ashford. Tonight, you gambled and lost and paid the casino fair and square,' he says with a shrug. 'Your agent, Lewis Orland, has gambled and he lost… against my boss. So, therefore, he needs to pay… fair and square. All you need to do is sign these documents, and your career will be at a place it has never reached before. The sky will be the limit.'

This guy is very good at what he does, and I can see why his boss, whoever he might be, has sent him. I feel his energy; his enthusiasm and I feel extremely tempted to sign. But I know that signing would spell danger, and I sense that they won't take *no* for an answer.

'How about I sleep on it and get back to you in the morning,' I say.

The man grunts, and is thoughtful for a moment, before making a call.

When the person at the other end answers- most certainly the boss- the man mumbles something in Russian and waits, listing carefully to the answer.

He then hangs up and stares at me.

'Mr. V is not keen on the idea.'

'That's a surprise,' I say.

'Don't make this difficult for us,' he says.

'Why now?' I ask.

'Why now?'

'Yeah. Why now? You've had four months to approach me when I was in England. So why come all this way?'

'Because your friend Lewis is a liar! Or shall I say your *dead* friend.'

'Dead?' I repeat, my heart thumping harder.

The man in front blurts something out in Russian, and the driver disapprovingly mumbles something back at him. Suddenly I notice three cars surrounding us, forcing the vehicle we are in to pull over.

It turns out they are the undercover narcotic police unit who had their eyes on Mr. V's men ever since they entered the country. The problem is, they also take me in too.

'As well as a large amount of cash, we found some class A drugs in the car,' says the detective, who introduced himself as Sarp. 'But lucky for you, you have already been proved innocent.'

A familiar face enters the interrogation room. To my surprise, It's the man with the grey eyes and short blonde hair, who has been following me like a phantom since the day I'd arrived.

'I'm Mustafa Hamza from narcotics,' he says. 'I'm aware you noticed me hovering around. But it wasn't you that I was following. It was them. They'd been following you for quite a while.'

'Are you aware of what they wanted from you?' asks Sarp.

Taking a deep breath, 'Yes, I do,' I reply.

'So, do we,' he adds. 'Bit of a sticky situation for you.'

'And where is your manager now?' asks Hamza.

'My agent?'

'Yes, your agent, Lewis Orland.'

'I don't know. They implied that he is dead, which I hope to God isn't true.'

'Sorry to hear that. There's nothing more we can do here, but charge them for the possession of drugs and the lady who assisted you to the car. I suggest you inform the authorities in the UK about Orland.'

'I will. Am I free to go?'

'They kidnapped you. Aren't you going to file a complaint against them?' asks Hamza.

'Of course, if you decide to, you'll have to testify in court,' adds Sarp.

I think about it for a moment. If this court case gets international exposure, my footballing license could be in jeopardy for not informing FIFA about the loan to Doğan. If Lewis is alive, he could lose his agency licence.

'It was hardly a kidnapping. I have no complaint,' I say.

Both the detective and Hamza turn and look at each other. I try to swallow but have a nervous lump in my throat.

'In that case, you are free to go,' says Sarp, eventually.

I head back home, feeling frightened and paranoid, knowing that Mr. V, whoever he is or wherever he might be, won't stop until he has my agency rights. I enter the apartment, constantly looking over my shoulder.

I call Lewis, but his phone is off. I don't sleep well, hoping he calls me, but he doesn't.

The following morning, I call Cliff Robson and get put through to Bec, his secretary.

'He's out and not taking calls,' she explains.

'Listen, Bec. I need to talk to him. It's about Lewis.'

'Lewis, your agent?'

'Yes.'

'He's been out of touch for a while. Mr. Robson tried to get in touch with him, but his phone is always off. We thought maybe he's over there with you.'

'No, he hasn't called me for a while now.'

I thank her and hang up, with the worst imaginable scenarios flashing through my mind.

8

DAVID Parmer, who always had an interest in football, has been a borderline Manchester United fanatic from a young age. Still, after seeing a different side to the game, gradually, the excitement started wearing off. Graduating with a first in law at the University of Bristol, he found himself getting involved with the dark side of sports law and now only takes on sports cases, most of which are up against the likes of UEFA, FIFA and other sports organizations.

I called David a couple of times yesterday, but each time it went to voicemail. Then I vaguely remembered he never did answer his phone on Sundays. So, this morning I try my luck again, and this time he picks up right away. I catch him off guard, as we haven't spoken for over a year. He says that he hasn't even heard about my injury, let alone the move to Cyprus.

'They kept that one quiet,' he exclaims.

'There's a reason for that,' I reply. 'I'm not even sure if it's safe to talk.'

'I'll leave that at your own risk, but I'm swamped with rouge cases as it is.'

I explain the whole story to him: how I got injured and needed urgent surgery and how at midseason, when I recovered, I ended up on loan to a club named Doğan Türk Birliği in Northern Cyprus. I also add that the main reason Lewis insisted on me coming here was to ensure I'd become match fit for next season.

But the truth of the matter is that I'd be hidden from a Russian mob that's after my agency rights, which Lewis gambled away in a lousy game of poker. And now there's a chance he's dead.

'That's tragic, Andrew. I don't know what to say. So, I'm guessing this is an S.O.S call?'

'You can say that. What do you recommend? I feel whoever this Mr. V is, won't stop until he's my representative.'

'You'll need to terminate your contract from Lewis,' he warns. 'That way, anything he's signed will be worthless.'

'So, who will be my representative?'

'Not me, that's for sure. I have enough enemies as it is! Don't need anymore,' he says, clicking his lips, then adds, 'You will.'

'I will?'

'You will automatically become your own representative once the contract with Lewis has been terminated. Just think about it. It will give you some freedom and you can use it to your advantage.'

I stop and think. I have no idea what is right or wrong at this moment in time. I can't imagine many of the agents getting their players into this kind of situation. Lewis has no one else to blame but himself. I agree with terminating my contract from him and becoming my own representative. I cannot say that I am not worried about him. But I do feel extreme anger and disappointment.

David tells me a secure address is needed. He says that he has an acquaintance that is a solicitor who has her law firm out here. He says he will get their address and call me back.

Suddenly the thought of being my own agent makes me feel uneasy like I'm drowning in deep and dark waters. I feel panic and anxiety set in.

Ten minutes later, he calls back.

'The name is Esra Özberk Law Firm. It's directly opposite the courts. DHL Express should have the documents delivered by Friday. You need to sign them and send them back. Mrs. Özberk will give you a call when the parcel arrives,' he says.

That evening I try to forget about work and meet Peter and Ahmet at a local bar named Papageno located near the main roundabout at the entrance to the city. I decide it's best not to mention anything about becoming my own agent and keep away from Lewis' disappearance, but that plan goes down the drain.

'I'm going for an Efes draft,' says Ahmet.

'A gin and tonic for me,' says Peter.

'A gin and tonic? That's a girl's drink,' Ahmet mocks him.

'Well, I wouldn't mind sharing it with her then,' Peter jokes back. 'Seriously though, the derby is coming up, I don't need the extra calories. And beer gives me a bloated stomach.'

'When you put it that way, it sounds wise. What are you having Andrew?'

At this stage, I'm miles away, still thinking about Lewis.

'Andrew?' Ahmet tries again.

'Andrew is having a dream,' Peter jokingly cuts in.

'Yes, sorry. I'll have a Miller.'

Papageno gets overcrowded with locals. And soon, I realize why. At the other end of the pub, a band starts plays Turkish rock music. A tremendous buzz arises as many of the customers sing along to one of the songs. My evening only gets better when I see Aysha sitting with two of her friends a couple of tables down from us.

'What are your plans for next season?' Ahmet asks. 'I heard that Alp wants you for another season.'

'That's one question I can't answer.'

'The reason why I ask is that I overheard him chatting with Robson today. He's having trouble contacting your agent.'

'He hasn't mentioned anything to me yet.'

'Is there a problem?'

'I wouldn't say it's a problem, but a slight change.'

'What do you mean by slight change?' asks Peter.

I sigh. 'I am now my own boss,' I say.

'Really? What happened to your agent?'

'We parted ways.'

'Why?' they both ask.

'Long story,' I say, relieved to see the waiter come to the rescue with the drinks.

I quickly change the subject, and it works, as for the next half an hour Peter rages on about his football career, how he is the hero of his town and to this day is still remembered at school. I can sit here all night, pretending to listen to him over the loud rock band- as long as Aysha keeps subtly glancing over once in a while.

Everyone receives the *stare* sometime in their life- and returns the *stare* too. What I mean by this is the hungry, passionate look you get (or give) to someone when they've fallen head over heels for you. But it's not at all intentional. Every time Aysha looks over, my heart beats faster- and with what Peter had said that time at the house party about her having a fiancé- at the same time, it sinks too. Yes, with her looks, she controls the way I feel. I try not to show too much interest, but it certainly is a challenge.

When Peter's phone rings, he excuses himself to go outside to talk, and Ahmet goes to the toilet, I see this as an opportunity to go over to Aysha's table for an innocent *hello*.

'It's been a while since I saw you,' she says, smiling. 'How are you?'

'Very well.'

'This is Andrew. He plays for Doğan,' she introduces me to her friends, Selmin and Ayla.

'Is that so?' says Selmin, who looks a bit gothic, a million miles from how Aysha looks. She doesn't sound convincing if anything somewhat pretentious, as if she already knows who I am.

68

'You ready for the big game on Saturday?' she asks, puffing on a thin cigarette.

'Ready as I'll ever be.'

'I didn't realize Turkish rock music was your thing,' says Aysha.

'Actually, I'm enjoying it,' I laugh.

'I hardly ever listen to this kind of stuff at home. I don't think anybody here does,' explains Ayla, who wears glasses, has a ponytail, and appears to be more intellectual than her chubby gothic friend sitting next to her.

'Maybe people prefer to listen to it live,' adds Selmin.

'I never had you down as a beer drinker,' I tell Aysha.

'That could be because I broke up with my fiancé a couple of days ago,' she says. 'It's the best way to get my mind off things.'

'I'm sorry to hear that,' I say, trying not to sound happy, but feeling a gush of joy.

'Don't be. I'm kind of relieved,' she answers.
We look into each other. Although it only lasts for about five seconds, it feels much longer.

'By the way, are you interested in classical music? There is a concert at the Abbey in Bellapais Thursday evening and Selmin has dropped out, so there's a spare ticket up for grabs,' she explains.

'Sure, he can have mine,' says Selmin.

'Are you sure?' I ask. 'I mean, I don't mind paying for it.'

'This one's such a gentleman,' she mutters, rolling her eyes.

'Consider it a gift,' smiles Aysha.

'Thank you.'

69

'So, see you there at half seven Thursday evening then?'

'Sounds good.'

I've never been into classical music. Some opera maybe, and that's thanks to Pavarotti's *Nessun Dorma*. For me, it's always been rock music.

When travelling on the bus to an away game, or sometimes after training while lying in bed, I find nothing more inspirational than putting on my *Bose* headphones and busting some Iron Maiden or Pink Floyd, depending on how I'm feeling at that moment in time.

But if a classical concert at an ancient Gothic church will get me closer to Aysha, then so be it!

9

IT'S been one hell of a week so far, with a cocktail of emotions. After training on Thursday, I notice a missed call from a local number. I call back as I stroll to the car. A lady answers. She introduces herself as Zehra, who is Esra Özberk's secretary.

The documents have arrived for signing. Never in a million years would I have thought I'd be terminating Lewis's contract to become my own representative.

Parking at the old Baldöken car park near the city centre, I make my way across the road from the courts, where the majority of the law firms are.

It doesn't take long to find Esra Özberk's Advocate office. A young lady sat behind a wooden desk, is lost in her iPhone. She looks up and instantly guesses who I am.

'Hello, Mr. Ashford. Miss Esra Özberk will be with you in just a couple of minutes,' she says.

Judging by her voice, she's Zehra, the girl I'd spoken to on the phone earlier. I sit and wait in the reception, staring at the top of her head while she entertains herself on her phone for fifteen minutes. Then eventually, I get called in and find myself comfortably seated on a dark-green leather Chesterfield sofa, facing Esra, behind her large mahogany desk.

She reminds me of Mrs. Price, one of my schoolteachers from years ago, who marked exam papers through her half-frame reading glasses. Esra wears the same, if not similar, as she scans the paperwork in front of her. After about two minutes, she looks up and forces a grin.

'Everything seems to be in order,' she says.

This is not the type of work they are used to out here. Eighty per cent of the lawyers on the island typically deal with divorce and property cases (in that order).

After all, the top level of any sport in Northern Cyprus is semi-professional, and if an athlete shines through at a higher standard, then the obvious place for them is the mainland (Turkey) or the South.

In 2003 the border opened for both sides to cross over. Mehmet Ali Talat took over from Rauf Denktaş (the founder of the Turkish Republic of Northern Cyprus, TRNC) as President in 2005, further easing relations with the south. Hundreds of Turkish Cypriots now cross over daily to work in the south, and therefore this gave players from the north a rare opportunity to play in the Greek Cypriot League.

'Brave of you to become your own representative,' states Esra. 'You must have solid contacts at other clubs.'

I sigh. The truth is, I haven't. Nevertheless, I do have friends and acquaintances playing on a professional level, who, I'm sure, could point me in the right direction. There are hungry agents out there who are always fishing for fresh players. I admit that I'm not young as a footballer, but I'm established and have plenty of life in me yet. Yes, there will be a lot of questions asked why I chose Northern Cyprus midway through the season, and the truth is I didn't have much choice.

I sign, with Zehra being witness to my signature. Esra stays quiet, but suspects there's something wrong- and she has every reason to- even if David hasn't given too much away. Why would a professional footballer playing in the second competitive league in England come here to a club that isn't recognized by FIFA and then suddenly decide to become his own agent?

She assumes I'm in hiding- a perfect place to hide. The British government doesn't recognize Northern Cyprus as a state, so the Home Office cannot agree on an extradition treaty. Although most cases are propaganda and exaggerated by the media, because there is no extradition treaty, the country attracts certain people who want to distance themselves from any attention from the British authorities. It suddenly dawns on me that if something has happened to Lewis, it won't do me any harm being out here away from the reach of the authorities.

'Do you get many clients from England?' I ask Esra on the way out.

'About ninety per cent of my clients are British,' she replies. 'Most come out here to buy properties.'

'It's a nice place.'

'Tourists fall in love with its beauty and peacefulness. It's not spoilt, and there's no commercialism here. I'd say it has one of the lowest crime rates in the world too.'

Mostly I agree with her, especially on the not spoilt part. I did feel at home and safe, until the encounter with the mob the other night, thanks to Lewis' stupidity.

Hoping that I've made the right decision, I head home to get ready for the big evening ahead.

The Polo pushes through the narrow Bellapais road that has no pavements, closely passing by the local shops, cafés and boutique hotels. I press hard on the accelerator, getting the most out of the stubborn engine, as the car inclines towards the Abbey on the steep road.

Aysha has warned me about arriving late. The car park outside the Abbey is small and gets packed quickly, especially in the evenings when special events are held. When I arrive, it is relatively full, with over an hour remaining before the concert starts.

I stroll around some of the souvenir shops opposite the Abbey. After a couple of minutes examining some authentic Turkish rugs hanging outside one of the shops, I notice Aysha across the road, waving me over, with Ayla standing next to her.

I get a peck on both cheeks. The moment is magical. Her perfume is just right: not too strong that it screams out, and not too diluted. She is wearing a white shirt with flower patterns running down the sides and black trousers, with shoes that have medium-heels on them. Today she has decided to let her hair down, and now it falls perfectly below her shoulders. I'm unsure whether to lean down and kiss her friend too, but she helps by frigidly reaching her hand out and shaking mine. Not even a grip, so it feels like **clutching a dead fish**. Evidently, the choirgirl isn't used to hanging around men.

'Have you eaten?' asks Aysha.

'No, I haven't.'

'Great! I've reserved a place at Kybele.'

Kybele is part of the abbey building, which is over eight hundred years old. As the evenings are chilly, we sit indoors, instead of its impressive garden.

'I'm looking forward to the concert,' I say as we take a seat in the crowded restaurant.

'Me too,' replies Ayla. 'The violinist is a friend of mine. We went to the same school.'

Aysha and I both ignore her, lost in each other's eyes. She raises a slight smile. A smile that says that she's happy that I came. I return her smile. *Likewise.*

We order steaks with salad and a bottle of **rosé**. An excellent way to get the evening started. As it's a concert night, the service is rushed but my steak is cooked to perfection: Medium-to-rare for me. Well-done for the girls. It goes down well with the wine. Aysha and I hardly talk as much as Ayla. Maybe it's her self defence mechanism of playing gooseberry.

As the concert time nears, we take our places inside the Gothic church. It's packed, and there are no spare seats. Eventually, a trio (two ladies in their mid to early thirties and a middle-aged gentleman in a suit) walks on stage and start

75

performing Beethoven's Op. 1 No. 3. I am genuinely bewildered at how good they are. The beautiful young lady leading on the grand piano is very talented. Another lady follows her lead on the violin, who I'm guessing is Ayla's old school friend and a tubby man, with a red face, joins them on the cello. Then without further ado, they go onto the next piece, the audience applauds. Usually, I would get bored after about twenty minutes, but not tonight. Not in this magical venue with these musicians performing this magic music, echoing off the ancient stones. Whether Aysha is the reason I am unsure, but for two hours, I don't think about Lewis' disappearance or the mob. I feel free and safe.

'That was really good! They were brilliant,' I tell Aysha after it finishes.

'Yes, they were pretty amazing. But you aren't just saying that to be kind?' she smiles.

'Not at all. I enjoyed it,' I say and mean it.

When we walk out of the hall, Ayla goes off to congratulate her friend, giving me some time alone with Aysha.

'Come,' she says, locking her hand under my arm. 'I will show you something.'

We walk into the dark car park past the abbey, with the surrounding lights hitting its yellow stoned walls, giving it a golden appearance and head to the other end of the car park.

With a sigh, I look down, mesmerised by the view.

The glittering lights shine brightly in the darkness below. The city seems quiet and peaceful, while the reflection of distant lights dances within the calmness of the Mediterranean Sea.

'Whenever I come up here and look down at Kyrenia, I feel stress-free. It's as if everything is all right in the world,' she says softly.

'I suppose that's what home feels like,' I say, also feeling at home, if not as much as her.

We stand about a metre apart from each other. As much as I want to put my arm around her shoulder, I can't do it. Maybe it's too soon. Or perhaps I respect her too much.

Nevertheless, out of all the nights on the island, so far, this has been by far the best. Then Ayla comes, and the moment is short-lived. We say our goodnights and I go home with a big smile on my face.

10

March 8th

THE following morning, I go to meet Hasan Alp at his office. Before the Ottoman period, the ancient building, that's now the club headquarters with the yellow and navy-blue flag hanging out in front, was initially built by the Venetians, as was the neighbouring harbour. I give three firm knocks on the large wooden door and distinctly hear Alp call *Giriniz*[8].

The unusual office has a line of shelves encircling the walls protected behind glass with locks on them, with a variety of cups and trophies won in previous years.

'Andrew, I haven't been able to get in touch with Lewis,' he says, getting straight to the point. 'It's been a couple of weeks now.'

'That's the reason why I'm here. He's missing.'

Alp stops and has to think about it for a moment, 'What do you mean by missing?' he asks. 'Is he away on holiday?'

I explain everything to him in detail. How Lewis gambled away my footballing representation rights to the mafia in a game of poker, then organised for me to come out here on loan

---

[8] Giriniz: *'Enter' in Turkish*

78

when I'd recovered from injury, to keep me hidden. I also tell him that Mr. V's men had been spying on me but got caught by the narcotics squad while they were forcing me to sign a new contract in a car.

'I don't know what to do with this,' grunts Alp rubbing his eyes.

'There's one more thing you need to know,' I fire.

'What's that?' he asks.

'I've terminated my agreement with Lewis. So, therefore, I now legally represent myself,' I say, handing him the papers.

He takes them from me, and his eyes light up as he scans them.

'Lewis had recommended that your arrival here should be low key. I was led to believe that the main reason for it was because we are not a recognized club by FIFA. But as it turns out, the reason for it was the mafia. Just what was he thinking? These men were bound to catch up with you. He also led us to believe that we can't deal with Luton directly. So the loan money is going through him.'

'What do you mean?'

'We send the payment weekly to his account, and he passes it on, taking his share of the commission. But for a couple of weeks, there's been no confirmation that he's received our payment. I got a call from a Luton. They want their money, which is why we need to locate Lewis.'

I start feeling light-headed. I never dealt with the financial side before. I always saw myself as just the athlete who turns up to the training sessions, plays a weekend game, and an odd weekday cup match and gets his cheque through the post.

'I'll talk to Luton and get them the payment by other means. As for the last two weeks' payments, I'll see what they'll suggest,' he adds.

He then slumps back on his leather chair and looks deep into my eyes.

'We need you, Andrew. We have a chance to win both the league and the cup this year. And it's thanks to you.'

'As far as I'm concerned, I'm here until the end of the season. But Cliff needs to be informed that I've parted ways with Lewis.'

'I want you to call me right away if you hear from Lewis.'

'You'll be the first to know,' I tell him.

The weather is pleasant- pushing around the mid-twenties, so I decide to stroll along Kyrenia harbour. I jog down the stone steps and turn left, observing the yachts and fishing boats on my right as I pass them by. When I reached the centre, a fish restaurant with the name SET FISH, written in silver, catches my eye- a place that a couple of the lads had recommended. I head up the stone steps that lead to it.

There are about ten tables outside, and only three of them occupied by customers who (like me) decided to come for an early lunch. A waiter wearing a welcoming smile shows me to a table and hands me a menu. I thank him and glance through it.

I then call Aysha, who didn't expect to hear from me so soon and seems happy to do so.

'I'd like to thank you again for the magical evening last night,' I say.

'You're welcome. I enjoyed it, too,' she replies. Great response!

'I know it's short notice, but how about lunch?'

'That's so sweet of you, but I can't do lunch. How about a coffee later on?'

'Sounds good. By the way, I'm at Set Fish in the harbour and just scanning the menu. Any recommendations?' I ask.

'I'd go for the white grouper,' she says. 'They do that well.'

I thank her, and after a couple of goodbyes, we hang up.

The waiter walks up to the table and pours some water.

'Anything else to drink, sir?' he asks.

'Water is fine.'

'Have you decided on what you would like to eat?'

'I can't see it on the menu, but please may I have a white grouper? A friend's recommendation.'

'Yes, that won't be on the menu, but we serve it on demand. It comes with our special white cheese salad and Cyprus potatoes,' he explains, not jotting the order down and keeping it in his mind. I've noticed quite a few waiters in other restaurants here doing the same, and yet they seem to get the order spot on each time without missing a single dish.

I observe the colourful scenery of the charming harbour. Apparently, throughout the early 1800s, before the British occupation in 1878, Turkish and Greek Cypriots used this, then quiet harbour, for trading purposes. Olives, carobs, wheat, and even goats and donkeys were exported. Caiques (small wooden boats) were used to import cotton, silk, and other luxuries. Two storied buildings were then eventually erected. The bottom floors were typically used as warehouses and the top as residences. Those warehouses have now been converted to cafes and restaurants, but the second floors are still residences to this day, which overlook the harbour. Just like the one above Set Fish.

My phone rings. No number shows up on the screen. I answer and hear the clicking of lips and then a clearing of a throat.

'Mr. Andrew Ashford,' someone says on the other end.

'Yes?'

'Please listen very carefully. It is of paramount importance that you do so. I have an offer for you that would be very foolish to refuse,'

'Who is this?' I demand.

'I'm Mr. V. It's terribly nice to finally talk to you, Ashford,' he says somewhat politely, but at the same time patronisingly; those simple worlds giving me butterflies in my stomach.

'What do you want from me? Where's Lewis?' I ask, trying not to sound too frantic.

'All these questions. Now listen here. Southampton FC is interested in transferring you. They are looking for a backup striker for Miller. This is your chance for a big break… a chance to shine in the Premier League.'

'I'm *not* interested in doing business with you!' I snap.

'Well, in that case, I recommend you don't come back here.'

'Where's Lewis?' I try again.

'Lewis had some trouble with the heat in Mallorca,' he giggles.

'The heat?'

'Very unfortunate. That penthouse was beautifully decorated before the fire.'

Those words hit me hard, and I can barely breathe, let alone speak.

'Goodbye, Mr. Ashford. I've sent you a friend request on Facebook. I'll be waiting for a message from you to confirm the transfer!'

He hangs up.

A new friend request notification from the name *Noeweir Tuhide* flashes on the screen. Surely, he can't be foolish enough to send me a request from his official account. Of course not. I scan the profile. If I accept, I'll be his only friend. There is no profile picture, either. It's a new account, especially registered to keep tabs on me. I look at the profile name more carefully, and it dawns on me. Noeweir Tuhide is not an actual name, but a warning... *Nowhere to hide.* I don't accept the request. Not just yet. I keep it hanging along with thousands of others, mostly from fans that got hold of my account.

The waiter comes over with the plate of grilled white grouper, accompanied by a portion of potato wedges and a large bowl of salad, with traditional white cheese. As appetising as it looks, I've completely lost my appetite. With trepidation, I glance around, feeling paranoid as if I'm being watched.

I search the Internet for news updates on Mallorca and stumble upon a random article covering an apartment fire. It indeed is Lewis' apartment block. It says that there have been no casualties.

I take a deep sigh.

The waiter is watching me from a distance, looking proud of the dish, so I force myself to eat. The taste of the fish is truly astonishing, nothing like I've ever tasted. Aysha certainly has good taste. My appetite slowly returns, and I end up finishing the whole plate, even the Cyprus potatoes.

'Would you like tea or coffee?' asks the waiter as he picks up the empty plate.

I almost ask for a Turkish coffee and then stop myself. I promised Aysha that I'd have one with her. I message her, and a couple of minutes later, I receive a message saying that she is on her way to the harbour.

Parking her Range Rover Sport on the high rocky pavement on the steep road under Kyrenia Castle, she greets me with a smile, looking glamorous and positive as always. One of her traits I adore is how down to earth and caring she is. Very different from what I am used to. In fact, the complete opposite of what I am used to.

'Have you been before?' she asks, looking up at the overshadowing castle.

'I feel ashamed to say that I haven't.'

'Three months and you haven't been inside?'

'Nope.'

'Well, that makes you a true local,' she laughs, hanging her bag over her shoulder and locking the car door. 'It's only the tourists and students that seem to visit it.'

'It's the same with most places,' I say. 'I never went to the London Dungeons, for example.'

'Really? I have.'

'Yes, but you were a tourist,' I grin.

'Actually, a student,' she smiles.

We make our way up the steep curving steps leading to a bridge that leads to the castle's entrance. At the top of the steps rests a small cabin, displaying brochures, maps, and books. An elderly gentleman sits behind the desk and mumbles something in Turkish. Aysha says something back to him, and with a smile, he indicates towards the castle and says, 'Please enter.'

'Thank you,' I reply.

As we walk over the bridge, I ask Aysha. 'Free of charge?'

'Only for residents,' she says.

As we pass the bridge and enter a massive gateway, a strong smell of seawater hangs in the air. I can almost smell the fish swimming in the depths of the clear Mediterranean waters. After we enter, we come across an unusual sight that astounds me: a tombstone.

I stop to read to whom it belongs and what the story is behind it. The name reads *Admiral Sadık Pasha*. An important figure in Ottoman times that conquered Kyrenia in 1570.

'People were much shorter in those days,' states Aysha.

'Yes, that's right. They lived shorter too. If it were these days, the size of that tombstone would be for a child.'

We walk further in and approach a spacious courtyard. A large group of tourists is gathered around a tour guide who gives an introduction to the historic landmark.

'As you can see, we are at the harbour's east end,' he utters. 'This castle was first built by the Venetians in the sixteenth century... although a Roman chapel does lie within its walls dating back to the twelfth century. First, we will start by going to the shipwreck museum, which I know a lot of you are looking forward to.'

The impressed tourists smile, mumbling amongst themselves, most with their camera phones on standby.

Aysha tugs on my arm. 'Let's see the shipwreck before they come and overcrowd the place,' she says.

The shipwreck museum is awe-inspiring, with items that were recovered from the actual shipwreck, all displayed behind glass. A diver discovered remains of the Greek merchant ship and its cargo some miles out in the Kyrenia waters in 1965. But what blows me away is the actual ship preserved in the next room.

I stand looking down with fascination at the 4th century BC vessel- one of the oldest to be recovered- in the freezing room, cooled by several air conditioners, keeping it well preserved.

We come out of the museum- which is now starting to fill with the tourists we saw out on the yard, their tour guide talking loudly over them, and we head up to the north side of the castle, overlooking the sea. The view is divine, with many tones and colours playing on the surface of the water, but

Aysha makes it more beautiful. Everything seems so natural and comfortable when she's around. Even the phone call from Mr. V is a distant memory. I do contemplate telling her the truth about how I ended up here, but I don't want to ruin this particular moment.

As a cool breeze blows from the sea, I notice that no one else is at this section of the building. Gathering up all my courage, I reach out and slowly wrap my arm around her shoulders, hoping I haven't gone too far too soon- but the feedback seems positive. She wraps her arm around my waist also, as we both gaze out to sea.

11

*March 9*th

PHONE in hand… gather up courage… take a deep breath in and then out, and then press the green button under Cliff Robson's name. It takes a couple of seconds to connect, and a lady answers.

'Mr. Robson's phone. This is Sarah Taylor, his assistant speaking. How may I help you?'

'Hello Sarah Taylor, I urgently need to speak to Cliff Robson,' I say.

'He's busy at the moment, but I can take a message-'

'Tell him that Andrew Ashford called.'

'Wait! Hang on-' she stutters, and Robson's voice cuts in.

'Andrew! I've meant to call you, but things have been manic here! Where the hell is Lewis?'

'I have no idea, but I think he may be in trouble.'

'What makes you think that?'

'You knew, didn't you?' I ask bluntly, ignoring his question.

'Knew what?'

'The *real* reason why Lewis was so persistent in sending me here. It was his idea, right?'

He pauses for a long moment, which makes me feel uncomfortable.

'Aye, I'm sorry laddie, there really was no other choice.'

'You should have told me the truth from the start!'

'We couldn't go into too much detail! Our priority was to protect you!'

'You mean your *priority* was to protect your reputation by sending me away! And still, that didn't quite go as planned. Did it?'

'Your destination was kept confidential! We need to track Lewis down.'

'That's why I called. To let you know that I'm now representing myself.'

He takes a deep sigh.

'That's a bit hasty.'

'I had a good long think about it.'

'How about Lewis? At least give him some time to turn up.'

'Did you hear about the fire at Lewis' penthouse in Mallorca?'

'No. What happened?'

'They say it was arson.'

There's another silence, this time a lot longer.

'And Lewis?' asks Robson, eventually.

'According to Spanish media, no bodies were recovered.'

'I need more information. I'll call Spain. So, as you are now representing yourself, we need to start talking about your future.'

'Maybe next week after the cup game,' I say.

'Sounds good. And when's this week's league game?'

'This afternoon… it's a derby.'

'Good luck!'

'Thanks.'

'And Ashford?'

'Yeah?'

'Keep up the good work.'

After the short and uncomfortable conversation with Cliff, I grab my sports bag and whiz down to the Doğan Türk Birliği club building, for the morning talk, prior to the derby match that is to be played against Türk Ocağı Limasol in the afternoon.

Everyone is quiet and hyped up for the clash that is nicknamed *Leymosun Derbisi*[9]. Just like Doğan, their black and yellow rivals, Türk Ocağı were formed by the Turkish Cypriots from Limassol. Doğan was formed in 1938, and Türk Oçağı fourteen years later in 1952.

Following the Turkish intervention in 1974, the Turkish Cypriots settled north and the Greek Cypriots to the south. A United Nations buffer zone divided the country. As most of the Turkish Cypriots from Limassol settled in Kyrenia, both clubs were also relocated here and share the same stadium: *20 Temmuz Stadı*, which means 20th July Stadium (commemoration of the intervention).

---

[9] Leymosun Derbisi: *The Limassol Derby*

90

'Today's game is not like any other,' reminds Remzi, with Ahmet translating for him. 'You are all aware of its importance. The last game against them was disappointing. The fans cannot deal with another result like that.'

'What was the score at the first game?' I whisper to Peter, who is sitting next to me.

'Three-one…you don't remember?'

'Wasn't here. I came mid-season, remember?'

'Oh yeah. My bad.'

'Erase that game from your memories,' continues Remzi. 'We are now a lot stronger. We have a solid strike force up front,' he looks at me for a split second and then continues, 'And what's more important, we are now playing more as a unit!'

Since my arrival, this has been the loudest crowd by far. The noise from the stands is incredible and it feels like a true derby game.

However, I notice how most the players from both the teams seem to know each other very well, probably from a very young age- a reminder of how small this place is. I get goosebumps when I hear the chanting of my name… *Ashford goal goal goal! Ashford goal goal goal!*

'Pressures on you, brother,' smiles Peter, as he tightens his laces.

'I'm used to it,' I reply, uncertain if I sound at all convincing.

As we run out, we are greeted with flares, bells, drums, and the blowing of horns. After a quick team photo by half a dozen cameras, we win the coin toss, which gives us the advantage to start the game.

Türk Ocağı wins the ball instantly- thanks to Doğan's sloppy passing- and goes on the attack- determined to get that early goal- but their shot on goal is just as sloppy and it goes out for a goal kick.

Türk Ocağı are about to start another attack when my nerves get the better of me, and I slide for the ball, taking out the player with it. The result of the reckless tackle is a yellow card- a decision I cannot argue.

A red-faced Remzi hysterically yells for the midfield to fall back and help with the defending. I eagerly wait near the halfway line like a lonely schoolboy at the playground who none of the other children wants to play with.

Ferdi, a tall central defender, outruns one of their strikers to get the ball- using the advantage of his unusually long legs- and chips it high towards me. I let it bounce once and do a quick take of the area ahead. Realizing the opposition has committed so far forward, I notice only one defender hanging back. Only having him and the keeper to get past, I sprint with the ball, but at this point, I am at an awkward angle to shoot and only two rational options present themselves. One is to shoot to the keeper's left and pray it sneaks in by defying physics, and the other is to play to the winger running in from the right. The winger Taşkın was the one who never passed to me in training because I was new- because he didn't know me- and because he preferred passing to his buddies instead. This guy has barely spoken to me since I came.

There always has to be one in the team! He has one of those patronising faces that I'd gladly punch. Now he is through on goal and bound to score if I pass to him.

At school, Mr. Hignall, the P.E. teacher, used to say that good passing is the key to a team's success during the five-a-side games. With good passing comes good possession, and with good possession comes goals. It's what I always based my play on. Remembering those words that were once drummed into me, I tap the ball towards Taşkın, who places it out of the keeper's reach, into the back of the net. The crowd erupts. Taşkın runs towards them to celebrate his moment of glory, followed by the team, who scrum around him (myself not included). I jog back to the halfway line watching the exaggerated celebration. A few players come up to congratulate me too. Unexpectedly, Taşkın also comes up and thanks me.

'It's a passing game,' I say. He looks into my eyes with some shame, knowing exactly what I'm talking about.

This one's in the bag. There's nothing that can go wrong, I think to myself in the second half and I feel like a fool in doing so.

A slick pass from Adil to Peter, then from Peter to Hasan, who acrobatically skips past an opponent, and passes it into an empty space, for me to run onto. I find myself one on one with the keeper, when a sharp pain stops me as the studs of one of their defenders dig into my ankle like a dagger, knocking me flat on my face.

The referee blows the whistle. I slowly get up and try to relieve the pain by shaking my lower leg, content with the penalty decision.

Booing arises from the stands as players from both teams surround the referee in anger. He ignores them, marches towards me while indicating a diving gesture, and shows me a red card. Looking on in disbelief, I hear Remzi hysterically yelling from the sideline- his voice going up a few octaves every passing second.

'Wasn't a bloody dive!' I argue, facing the first-ever red-card of my life.

Ignoring me, he points to the changing rooms. I bring my sock down and expose my red ankle, with scrapes showing on the bruised skin. He doesn't even acknowledge it. But then again, when do they ever?

Tail between legs, I take the walk of shame past the stands and towards the changing rooms for an early shower. The Doğan fans give me a standing ovation, as the Türk Ocağı ones- at the other end- mock me by cheering with joy at my misfortune.

What makes things worse is that we have to settle for a point as they score ten minutes from time with the game ending all square. Çetinkaya has now gone four points clear at the top of the league with only eight games remaining. Remzi is sympathetic towards me as he saw the foul but is still raging on about the awful decision.

'We've been robbed,' he hisses. 'I won't keep quiet about this! I'll talk to Alp and suggest he contacts the football federation first thing Monday morning!'

We gather around him in the small changing room with his towering figure overshadowing us. He stares at the ground, his red eyes full of anger. One decision that changed the course of the game has transformed him into a completely different person compared to the calm and collective one who gave us the half-time talk.

'Taşkın… Adil, you were both asleep today! The wingers are supposed to make the team fly! You might have scored Taşkın, but during the second half, you seemed lost!'

'After going a man down, they placed four attacking midfielders and the defence kept passing up the centre,' mumbles Adil, while Taşkın just rolls his eyes and shakes his head in disapproval, not saying say a word.

The coach completely ignores Adil's comment and says, 'We should have won today. Even with the biased ref, we should have scored more!'

He speaks nonstop for fifteen minutes, giving his most prolonged post-match talk so far. I find it very repetitive. And after a while, Ahmet gives up translating for Peter and me.

My mind wanders to Aysha. I wonder what she is doing this evening.

Suddenly I feel energised, even after playing a seventy-something minute game. I type a quick message, *Dinner tonight?*

It's not long until she replies, *Sorry about red card- unfair decision. Dinner sounds good! Where and what time?*

I look for Ahmet, but he's disappeared. I don't blame him as a few of the players have been loudly arguing amongst themselves after Remzi's talk.

Hurriedly, I escape the noisy changing room and find Ahmet standing near the car park, talking to some men while sipping on a carton of *ayran*[10]. I ask him if he can recommend a romantic restaurant for evening dining. He tries to get it out of me who the lucky lady is. But I keep schtum. At this stage, I don't think anyone associated with the club would be ready to hear I'm dating Alp's daughter. Especially, straight after she's broken up from her fiancé.

'Try the Fez in Çatalköy,' he says. 'They have an English pub menu and a romantic atmosphere.'

I thank him and book a table for two for 8 pm. Aysha seems happy with the decision.

---

[10] Ayran: *A Turkish drink made from yogurt, water and salt.*

12

LOOKING through tabloid newspapers has always been somewhat of a pastime since my early teens. I find most of the news worthless and cringe-worthy, but still can't seem to live without them. I hold the phone close to my face, stunned by what I see on the front page, as a large picture of a young Lewis Orland stares back at me with a grin on his face. The title reads BRIT MISSING IN SPAIN. Looking at his old picture takes me back ten years.

'Perform your best today. There will be a handful of agents watching,' Harry Joyce, Stoke Youth Academy coach had warned, during the final training session before a rare friendly game against the Chelsea Under 16s.

You can ask me the final score of that game and I won't be able to tell you, but what I do remember is that I scored a real screamer- a diagonal volley from the edge of the box- what was to be the jumpstart to a professional career. It wasn't the goal so much that impressed Lewis, but the way I positioned myself. I received the pass and moved to the side, taking out two defenders before placing it in the back of the net.

A mature bit of footwork coming from a teenager, Lewis had thought at the time.

'That was impressive, lad. How about a trial down at Luton?' he had asked.

'Sure,' I'd replied.

'But make sure you talk to your parents first.'

And that was how our footballer–agent relationship began. He always told me that I'd eventually move up to the Premier League and that I should trust him. Although I wanted to, deep down, I never fully did.

Lewis Orland, 52, was last seen going into his apartment in Majorca last week, as fire broke out the following day, due to a suspected arson attack. However, Spanish authorities have confirmed that there have been no fatalities or injuries resulting from the incident. The investigation continues.

I feel grim, but still, have some hope that Lewis is okay. Hope that I hold onto because there has been no evidence of any fatalities. There is also hope because Lewis is a calculating and cunning character. The only thing that keeps me from losing my mind is Aysha. I feel a sudden onset of guilt because I am thankful for Lewis' gambling habits. I would have never ended up here and met her if it wasn't for his addiction.

I take a long shower, which lasts over twenty minutes. By my standards, that's almost a lifetime. Then I shave, carefully sliding the blade over every area covered with stubble, being extra careful not to miss any spots or to cut myself. Usually, shaving is in my morning routine, but not today. Tonight is my first official date with Aysha, and it will just be the two of us. There will be no choirgirl or gothic-girl playing gooseberry.

My hair takes another quarter of an hour, as I work the wax onto each strand, with only ten minutes to spare to choose what I will wear. A white Hugo Boss polo-neck shirt and navy-blue Armani trousers seem perfect for the occasion. I slip on a jacket and a pair of dark-blue trainers, jump into the Polo and make my way to the Fez.

I slowly head towards Çatalköy through the Saturday night traffic. There are a lot of cars parked on the side of the road. I later learn that they are the ones that couldn't find parking places at the Cratos Hotel, where a famous pop singer from Turkey is performing. After passing the Cratos, the traffic opens up, and I arrive at the Fez in no time.

The old Mediterranean building has been given an internal makeover inspired by a classic English pub. The wooden bar stretches to the dining area, and above on the corner wall, a television airs rugby on Sky Sports 1.

'YOU'RE THROUGH… YOU'RE THROUGH… YOU'RE THROUGH!' calls a man loudly in an Irish accent, almost spilling his pint of lager as I walk past.

The dining area is full. A sudden feeling of hunger hits me hard as the food on the tables materialises in front of my eyes. Although the burgers look appetising, what excites me is the roast lamb. Since coming here, I hadn't had a nice roast meal.

Aysha sits, lost deep inside her phone, wearing an elegant silver top and black trousers. She looks more stunning than ever before. When she notices me, she stands and puts out her hand to shake mine. We lock hands tightly for a moment, lost in each other's eyes. I notice they are a dark tone of green with a distinctive shape as if perfectly drawn by a manga artist. Her lashes are naturally long, so therefore not much mascara is needed. In fact, because of her natural beauty, I can only imagine that she only needs to apply a small amount of makeup, if none at all.

'You're such a rebel,' she says with a smile.

'Rebel?'

'Red-card.'

'I'm still extremely annoyed about that.'

'So is everyone else. They had high hopes for the cup game against Çetinkaya.'

It suddenly dawns on me that I will be suspended for the cup final because of the red card.

I sigh deeply. 'They should introduce some kind of VAR[11] system here with decisions like that! That was a clear penalty!'

'That's debatable,' she replies.

'Debatable, huh?'

She smiles and replies, 'I'm only pulling your leg, silly. There was definite contact there. The defender should have been given the red.'

'Well, it's good of you to think so,' I say jokingly and we both burst into laughter.

'Interesting choice by the way,' she says, looking around. 'Haven't been here in ages.

'It's my first time. I'm glad you approve.'

---

[11] VAR: Video Assistant Referee

'They do a good roast.'

'It's been a while since I had one. Probably the last time was at my mum's for Christmas.'

'Do you ever get homesick?'

'Been a long time since I left home. Even when I was living in England, I was far from my folks. Must have been difficult for you to be away from your family when you went to England.'

She smiles and then looks down. 'I was sent to boarding school in England at the age of eleven.'

'Harsh,' I say. *No wonder her English is so good*, I think to myself.

'Was a bit… back then there wasn't much choice. Now there are a handful of public schools here to choose from. Before, there were just state schools.'

'What did you do after boarding school?'

'So, I took my A-levels and went on to study architectural engineering at London College.'

'Is that what you do now… design buildings?'

'I certainly do.'

'You didn't want to go into the hotel business like your father?'

'Not at all. I'm doing something that I enjoy.'

I wonder what Alp would think if he were to find out that I was on a date with his daughter. I almost ask her, but then decide not to.

Overall it's an enjoyable evening, which gives me a chance to get to know Aysha better. She admits that her family is one of the wealthier ones living in Kyrenia. They are full of ambition, so much so they didn't mind parting from their children at a young age sending them far away overseas to give them the best education possible. I also find out that Aysha has a younger brother, Ali, who works as a lawyer in a firm in central London. Her mother is a typical old-fashioned Cypriot housewife, who fell in love with Hasan at a young age when they were both at college. It wasn't long before they got engaged and she ended up waiting for him to finish university and military service before getting married. Aysha is so engrossed in telling me about her life story that she hardly gets a chance to ask about mine, which I am okay with, as I don't want to spoil a beautiful evening by mentioning to her that my father had died five years ago, due to cancer.

Twenty minutes after ordering, the food arrives. The roast is delightful; the lamb smells divine, complemented by golden oven-baked potatoes and freshly boiled vegetables, gravy, and a garnish of mint sauce on the side. Aysha has gone for the fish and chips, which also looks good and very similar to what you would get served in Britain.

After we finish our mains, she looks up and smiles cheekily.

'How 'bout sharing an apple pie?' she asks flirtatiously.

'Half an apple pie can't hurt,' I say.

'Would you like that with custard or ice-cream?' asks the waiter.

Aysha and I look at one and other and at the same time, call out, 'Custard!'

'Good choice,' says the waiter.

Her phone starts to ring- a call that will suddenly turn things from sweet to sour.

She glances at it and puts the caller on hold.

'Are you okay?' I ask, sensing her panic.

Stubbornly her phone rings again.

'Are you sure you don't want to get that?' I ask.

'Excuse me,' she says uncomfortably and heads outside.

The apple pie comes five minutes later, but I wait. I take my phone out of my pocket and try calling Lewis. My heart sinks when a voice message says that the number is no longer registered.

Approximately twenty minutes pass, I sense something is wrong. Over the music and the fast-talking rugby commentator I could have sworn I heard screaming outside the front door. Then distant shouting follows, coming from the car park. No one seems to notice over the noise. Even if they did, why would they care about screaming outside? As far as they are concerned, someone has had too much to drink. Springing up from my seat, I swiftly pace towards the front door, past the crowd of customers happily chattering amongst themselves, enjoying their drinks.

I'm faced with a shocking scene when stepping outside into the parking area. A tall man is tugging on Aysha's arm and trying to force her into a black BMW X6. Aysha is yelling in panic for him to let her go. I freeze for a moment and watch on in shock.

'GET IN!' he yells at her with his overgrown fringe falling over his eyes. He seems slightly out of place wearing a tuxedo and a black leather jacket over it, somehow giving him a patronising appearance.

'LET HER GO!' I cry.

He turns and looks at me grimly, still holding onto Aysha's arm tightly. He pushes her away and makes his way towards me.

'This is your entire fault, you ignorant *footballer*,' he snaps. 'Ever since you arrived on the scene, her character has changed!'

'No, Umut! The reason why my character has changed is that you slept with someone else!'

She's never mentioned this before, but now it makes sense why she's ended it with him. What a *rat*! How can anyone cheat on *her*?

He stops for a moment and glances back at her, then he growls and continues to pace towards me.

'Keep away from her you piece of dirt! She's already spoken for and can never stoop down to your level, footballer!'

'Wow, no need to get personal here, Umut… is it?'

'YOU DON'T TELL ME WHAT TO DO!' he barks. 'I know your type. You footballers are all the same. Especially you dirty foreign ones!'

He is now a couple of metres away and I smell the alcohol on his breath as he nears. Clenching his fist, he takes a swing at me, drunkenly punching the air, but missing my chin by inches. On the spur of the moment, as I try and defend myself, I take a swing back. My fist catches his jaw, and he comes crashing down to the ground.

'ANDREW!' Aysha screams with disapproval.

Now, a crowd of shocked faces surrounds the scene. Most are customers from the restaurant, as well as some passers-by. Aysha worriedly looks down at Umut and then glances at me.

'It was a reflex,' I explain.

She slowly nods pale with shock. On the ground, Umut groans in pain with his hands over his face as a man leans over him and tries to help him up. Sirens echo in the distance and it's not long before a police car rushes into the car park. I know this will not end well.

They talk to Umut first, who is now off the ground and pressing an icepack against his face. He doesn't look over once and is doing a great job playing the victim.

The two policemen then approach me.

'So, you punched him?' one of them asks.

'It was in self-defence,' I say.

'Answer the question. Did you punch him? Yes or no?' he asks.

Aysha tries to explain something in Turkish, but they don't seem interested in what she says.

'Yes, I did,' I say bluntly.

'You're coming with us. A complaint is being filed against you.'

'Is this necessary?' I ask. 'Look at him. He's all right. Plus, he went for me first, so I had to protect myself. He was trying to kidnap her! If anyone needs to be taken away, it's him!'

'In that case, she can file a complaint against him. But now you come with us.'

'He was trying to kidnap you! Tell them, Aysha!'

In shock, she stands still, tears running down her cheeks.

'Tell them!' I repeat.

'I'm sorry,' she breathes.

On the way to the police station, it occurs to me that everything might have been planned. Umut wanted me to retaliate. I recall seeing another guy talking on the phone, the same person who helped him off the ground. That's why the police arrived as fast as they did. It was all set up, and I fell straight into the trap. His message is clear: If I can't have her, then no one can!

I find myself in a small cell in the basement of the police station, a couple of doors down from Mr. V's men. The place is made of concrete, even the bed. It's dark with no windows, so day and night cannot be differentiated. What disturbs me most is the smell of sewage and mould.

Sobbing, screaming, even loud laughter echoes from the walls. I call out asking how long I'll be here, but no one is around, or they are close by and ignoring me. All my belongings, including my watch, have been confiscated; I have no idea how long I've been here. It feels like a couple of days, even though I know it was only one night.

A guard approaches the cell and unlocks the steel door.

'Follow me,' he grunts.

'Where are we going?' I ask, feeling anxious.

'Follow me,' he repeats.

I follow him up the stairs to the front desk, where to my surprise, Hasan Alp waits looking grim, pale and shattered as if he's been up all night.

I hang my head in shame and, under my breath, manage a quiet, 'Hello.'

He doesn't return the greeting and seems silent and upset.

'You are a lucky man. Mr. Alp had a word with the victim,' explains the chief police officer, standing next to him. The complaint has been withdrawn, so therefore the charges will be dropped. You don't go around hitting people!'

I nod but don't answer, as I know it wouldn't be wise to.

'I'll take you to your car,' sniffs Alp, while I retrieve my personal effects from a clear plastic container. The first thing he says to me, and it already feels like a grilling.

It will be one bumpy ride, I think to myself.

'I don't know how to thank you for getting me out of here. I appreciate it, but it won't be necessary. You've already done enough. I can make my own way to get my car,' I say as politely as possible, trying not to offend him.

'I didn't ask,' he says signalling me out to the car park.

Nervously I walk out and take a deep breath in, welcoming the fresh air into my lungs. I turn on my phone to check for any messages. Surprisingly there aren't any, not even from Aysha.

I place myself in Alp's silver Range Rover Vogue. I guess that the car is relatively new, as the smell of the leather is still fresh.

He winds down his window, grabs a cigar, takes it out the packet and lights it up while driving. I try and think of something to say to lighten the tension.

'Thank you again,' is all I can come up with.

He nods slightly and takes a deep puff, carefully directing the smoke out of the window.

'How's Aysha?' I ask.

'You keep away from her,' he says, uncomfortably.

'Mr. Alp, we didn't do anything wrong-'

'What were *you* doing having dinner my daughter, huh?'

'I swear I have no bad intentions. We get along.'

He turns and gives me a look. 'You go and get along with somebody else!'

I look at him and sigh not knowing what to say. His words are a knife to the heart and echo in my head for the rest of the day.

13

March 13th

SO far, it's been a miserable week. One I'd rather forget. Mostly I keep my phone turned off. I received a couple of missed calls and text messages from Aysha, apologising for the unfortunate events from last Saturday. But Hasan Alp has already made his feelings quite clear- and Alp is her father, who also happens to be my boss. I have no choice but to respect his decision and stay away from his daughter.

I don't return her calls or messages. She chose not to tell the police that Umut had tried to force her into his car, something I can't seem to get my head around. Not that it matters anymore. I feel relieved this incident took place sooner rather than later. I try to forget about her and the whole fight thing with her agro ex, but that's easier said than done.

As I'm suspended for the next game (thanks to the red card), I train alongside the reserves, supervised by a coach who looks younger than most of the players. Only a handful of them will be on the bench for the cup game on Saturday. Their hearts aren't really in it as they traipse around the field. Today the conversation revolves around hunting. As outdated as it might be, it appears to be a common hobby amongst the locals.

'Every Sunday morning, I get up at five in the morning to hunt,' says Halit proudly.

That's madness, I think, keeping the thought to myself.

'*Every* Sunday of the year?'

'Unfortunately not! The hunting season takes place between October and February.'

'So, what do you hunt?' I ask, jogging ahead.

'Partridges, pigeons… hares… çiklas[12]…' he replies, trying to catch his breath. 'Why don't you join us this Sunday?'

'I think I'll pass,' I say with a smile.

Remzi approaches the group, getting us to gather around him.

'Make sure you're prepared, as anyone of you can get a call-up,' he warns. 'You can suddenly find yourselves on the subs bench, ready to come on. So, no slacking! Even if you don't make it into the squad, you need to come to Nicosia on Saturday and support your friends. After all, this is the cup final. Afterward, you will be on the field collecting your medals!'

He turns and shoots me a stare.

'Ashford, that goes for you too!'

---

[12] Thrush: small bird

*   *   *

Depressed and homesick, I lie in bed with the lights off, listening to *Dark Side of the Moon* by Pink Floyd. It's not that it will help my situation, but at the moment it's the only music I can tolerate. It's 9 pm but feels a lot later. When the album ends, I decide to call my mother. She sounds ecstatic to hear from me.

'Darling, is everything okay?' she says.

'Yes mum, everything is okay. No need to worry about me. Seriously.'

'Well, do you blame me with Lewis still missing? It's all over the news, you know.'

'How's everything down your end? Any news?' I ask, changing the subject.

'Not really, dear... apart from aunt Anita's met someone nice, apparently,' she says with a giggle.

'Really? Isn't it a bit... you know... too soon?'

'Nonsense! It's been over a year since Barry died.'

'Barely. Just seems a bit quick.'

'Actually, I'm meeting the lucky man tomorrow. We're going out for lunch. Anita will introduce us. I'll tell you all about him later!'

'Looking forward to it.'

We say our goodnights. I decide it's best not to mention Mr. V.

* * *

March 16th

The kick-off time is 8 pm, so the game will be played under floodlights at the Atatürk Stadium in Nicosia, named after the former President and founder of modern Turkey, Mustafa Kemal Atatürk.

The stadium holds twenty thousand and is home to three teams: Yenicami (who we are playing tonight), Çetinkaya and a league-one team called Gençlik Gücü.

We get there an hour before kick-off. As I'm suspended for this one, I'll be watching from the stands. Ahmet hands me a free pass.

I approach the VIP entrance, where an elderly gentleman glances at the bit of plastic around my neck for a mere second and then nods, not looking at my face once. Entering, I make my way up towards the very top, where it's relatively secluded. Eventually, after forty minutes of entertaining myself on social media, the crowd erupts as both of the teams jog out onto the pitch.

Doğan are in their classic navy-blue and yellow striped shirts and Yenicami all in white. The captains shake hands, then the ref flicks the coin. We're ready to go!

Yenicami wins the toss and choice to kick off. Even after a quarter of an hour, the pace is slow, and neither team looks like scoring.

A well-dressed man in a shirt and tie enters the stands. Out of all the empty places up here, he sits one away from me. He looks and smiles, as if he is going to say something, then focuses back on the game.

'At the end of the day, it's all a big waste of time,' he says eventually.

I look at him. 'Sorry?'

'It turns into somewhat of an addiction, if you see what I mean. But at the end of the day, it's all a waste of time,' he repeats while following the game. 'I mean these teams are playing each other... and for what? The loser will get a pat on the back... if that... for being finalists... and the winner will win that tiny bit of silverware. And that's it.'

I nod, keeping my eyes on the game.

'I often ask myself what the point is when the International Football Federation simply doesn't want to know,' he continues. 'In other countries across Europe winning a game like this would have meaning... a place in a European competition. You know that better than anyone else. But just what is the point?'

I turn and look at him.

'So why doesn't anyone do anything about it?' I ask.

'Trust me, kid, I've tried,' he says, frowning in disappointment. 'I've spent the last twenty years researching and fighting for justice! I even went to the Court of Arbitration for Sport and the FIFA headquarters in Zürich on occasion!'

The crowd in the opposite stands cheer as Yenicami wins the game's first corner.

'So, do you think FIFA and UEFA could ever recognize the teams here?' I ask.

The ball bounces off the head of a Yenicami midfielder and makes its way into the Doğan goal.

'Bad bad defending,' he sniffs. 'The answer to your question is *No, I don't*. The politics just doesn't allow it.'

He shrugs.

'I haven't introduced myself. I'm Osman Esen,' he says, reaching out.

'Andrew Ashford,' I reply, shaking his hand.

'I know who you are. And it's an honour to have players like you playing in our country.'

I thank him.

'But I'll tell you something. The FIFA status claims it doesn't get involved with the politics in sports. And yet I've spent years and years trying to get them to implement this principle,' he explains, keeping his eyes on the field as Doğan launches its first dangerous attack.

'With no success?' I ask as Doğan's shot bounces off the woodwork.

'There has always been uncertainty. FIFA's position on this matter has always been somewhat ambiguous.'

'That's a shame, people here are passionate about football,' I add.

Esen turns and looks at me with glassy brown eyes.

'None of the young fans in this stadium or the players on the field can understand or feel what I feel. With my time at

Doğan, we travelled to places like Belgium and Germany to play pre-season friendlies, but never had a chance to play against the European teams, because of the embargo! There were teams cancelling games at the last minute, so those matches ended up as training sessions. Just imagine the disappointment! The let-down! And the shattered dreams of the players,' he says. 'There were times I couldn't sleep at night.'

'I'm sorry to hear that,' I say with sympathy.

Doğan desperately pushes forward again, with Peter passing the ball long towards the opposition's box, which reaches Hakan, who got given playtime in my absence today. Brilliant first touch of the ball- couldn't have done better myself- and he neatly places the ball past the keeper and into the back of the net.

'Superb!' cries Esen, clapping loudly.

'I hope that teams here will someday be permitted to participate in European competitions,' I say.

'It's ironic,' he chuckles. 'The FIFA slogan says *No to racism.* And yet if you are born in this country, it won't allow you or your team to participate in their competitions.'

Osman Esen turns out to be a fifty-five-year-old lawyer who once played for Doğan and ever since retiring from the game, has spent his time trying to get recognition for football in Northern Cyprus.

He doesn't say much after that and we both concentrate on the game. It ends all square and goes into extra time- with no goals- and then to penalties.

The atmosphere becomes tense as it always does with penalties. For the first time tonight, I am glad I'm not on the field waiting for the ordeal that will settle the game, with a fifty-fifty chance.

Doğan misses the first penalty, with the ball going wide of the post. It turns out to be a costly mistake, as Yenicami score all of theirs and wins the game 6-5, winning the *KKTC Süper Kupa*.

'Oh well,' says Esen disappointedly. 'Can't win them all.'

'No, you can't.'

'They're calling for you,' he says.

I see one of the assistant coaches signalling for me to come down and receive my silver medal (given to the team players who reached the final but lost).

Half-heartedly, I walk down to the pitch and join the queue of disappointed faces with their chins down, not speaking a word.

When it's my turn, the football association president hangs mine over my neck, congratulates me for helping the team reach the final, and with a half-hearted smile says, 'Your absence was felt tonight.'

14

A big bang wakes me up from my dreams. Irritated, I open my eyes as the heavy rain thumps against the bedroom window. I look at the time. It's only 1.27 am. Another loud bang follows, as lightning strikes, sending vibrations through the entire room and down my spine.

Lamely, I force myself out of bed and peep out of the window, as chilled air comes through the ledge, which awakens a distant memory from when I was just seven.

Like now, I was awoken by a loud noise in the early hours of the morning. I can't remember any rain, but what I do remember is the wailing of strong gales. And just like a moment ago, I got out of bed, or maybe at that age, I leapt out of bed and ran to the window to investigate. I remember standing in shock, staring down at the garden. I could hardly believe my eyes. My brand new swing- the one my late father had bought me for my birthday a couple of days earlier- was crushed under the tree that had fallen from next door.

I'd tried so hard to hold back the tears, but emotion always gets the better of you at that age. Every couple of seconds, thunder lit up the entire garden and my bedroom exposing the strength of nature with every flash that was followed by a bang.

Leaving the past behind, I return to the present and take one last glimpse out the window. The streetlights are off. It looks like the thunder has taken out the electricity. I take my phone off Flight Mode, allowing the train of messages to pour in. Most are trash, advertisements that I usually erase even before opening, but one, in particular, catches my eye, sent by Aysha at 22.43. It reads: *My dad wants to talk with you.*

Emitting a deep sigh, I lie back down and stare blankly at the ceiling, watching the entire room light up by the occasional flash of lightning. If Alp wanted to talk to me about football, he would send a message through either Ahmet or Remzi and certainly not through his daughter. This, I guess, is personal. So, what would Alp want to see me about? He had already made his feelings quite clear about his daughter being off-limits. Another grilling just wouldn't make sense. I try not to think about it, and my mind wanders to Lewis. There's still no news of his whereabouts. Every day that passes by is another day of hope evaporating. Rolling onto my side, I close my eyes, but can't bring myself to sleep. So much for a Sunday lie-in!

Eventually, I doze off and wake just past eleven. The sky has now turned a bright blue with no sign of those dark clouds from earlier. It's as if there been a change in season overnight, with the morning sun already drying up the dampness. Most of the rainwater from the floods has filtered into the ground. Now all that remains are a couple of puddles. I yawn and stretch, the back of my hand presses against something cold. It's my phone. Rotating my wrist at a challenging angle, I slowly grab it. It's still opened on the message that Aysha had sent earlier.

I stop and think for a moment, then reply, *About what?*

He will call you, she messages back five minutes later.

I take a long shower and then brush my teeth, keeping my phone close by at all times.

Although I've only been training with the reserves and didn't play in the cup final, somehow, I feel even more tired and more worn out than usual. I put it down to mental stress as opposed to physical.

Jumping into some shorts and throwing on a t-shirt, I stroll in to the kitchen and force myself to have a slice of buttered toast and a cup of black tea, but I have no appetite. I just sit at the table and wait for the club president to call.

The phone rings ten minutes later, just as I'm gulping down the last drop of tea. It's a withheld number, so I assume it's Alp, but when I answer, I get a nasty surprise.

'Mr. Ashford, I'm extremely disappointed in you,' exhales Mr. V.

'What do you want?' I ask, feeling my blood pressure rising.

'I was expecting an answer by now. As your new agent, I demand some respect.'

'Get lost!' I snap.

'Very well, your choice,' he says. 'But I can see that you haven't thought things through. Because if you had, you would have seen how evil Lewis is… was. You think your leg injury was purely coincidental? What kind of agent pays for his player to get injured? If I were you, I'd think things through again, Mr. Ashford. An opportunity like this is rare.'

I keep silent, too stunned to answer. Could my injury be Lewis' doing? Not that Mr. V is trustworthy either and is known for playing mind games. But the more I think about it, the more coincidental it seems.

'Anyway, I expect an answer from you soon,' he sniffs. 'Are you on board? Or will you waste your life away? Tick-tock, tick-tock.'

With anxiety, I throw on a jacket and go for a very long walk towards Alsancak, a town west of Kyrenia, where there is a bay, known as Escape Beach. Although I don't time myself, it must take at least two hours to reach.

Escape Beach was previously known as *Çıkarma*, which means *extraction*. In 1974, it was here that the Turkish army had landed and set foot on the island.

As I walk, the wheels in my brain start turning. I begin to feel paranoid as if I'm not wanted in the team anymore. Even Peter, who I am closest to, was acting cold on the bus to Nicosia. He hardly said a word all journey. After all, he did warn me to keep away from Aysha, so I suppose I have no one to blame but myself.

Sitting myself down on a single rock, I look out towards the placid sea displaying different tones of grey, green, and blue.

For the first time in days, I start feeling calm and relaxed. The misty outline of the mountains in Turkey is visible on the distant horizon. Unfortunately, the therapy does not last long because of my phone ringing. Like earlier, the number is withheld. I blankly stare at the screen for a moment and take in a deep breath. I really can't be dealing with this shit again.

'What do you want?' I say coldly (thinking that it's Mr. V again) but surprised to hear Hasan Alp's voice on the other end.

'Ashford? Are you okay?' he asked, sounding a little astounded by how I rudely answered the phone.

After receiving that horrid call from Mr. V, I cannot believe it completely skipped my mind that Alp was due to call.

'Sorry, I thought you were someone else,' I say.

'Yes, yes… I gathered that,' he says. 'Meet me at The George at five. And don't be late.'

He hangs up and I glance at the time on my phone's screen. It reads 14:25, which gives me just under three hours to make it home, shower, and then drive to The George. Burning rubber, I sprint back and arrive at the flat breathless and sweaty in just under two hours.

I get there a couple of minutes before five. Alp is already sitting outside, puffing a large cigar, and drinking cappuccino.

His face is expressionless as he points at an empty chair for me to sit on.

As always, The George is full of English customers who are mostly residents. Sky Sports 1 is airing a live Premier League game between Chelsea and Spurs on a couple of the screens. On another is a rugby game between Australia and South Africa.

'What are you drinking?' Alp asks.

'I'll just have a soda,' I reply.

'How've you been? Got over the trauma of the other night?'

'I'm okay. I'd like to thank you again for bailing me out.'

'You were going to be standing in front of a judge the following morning. Should count yourself lucky,' he says, as he puffs on the cigar, and a couple of seconds later exhales out a large cloud of smoke.

'I really appreciate it,' I say.

He notices me looking at the cigar and smiles.

'It's a bad habit. The wife gives me an ear full about it, but I have no intention of giving up.'

'One soda here,' he calls to one of the waiters, who nods and rushes into the bar.

'I disturbed you on a Sunday, but this is a matter outside work. An important matter.'

My soda comes. Alp waits for the waiter to move away before continuing.

'I had a chat with Aysha, and she explained the whole incident from the other night. I hate to say this, but she seems fond of you, Ashford.'

Caught off guard, I try to keep a straight face.

'She did?' I ask, fighting back a smile.

'Once I had a chance to listen to her side of the story, I think I owe you a *thank you* for protecting her.'

'You're welcome.'

'But, as a father, I need to be sure that my daughter will be safe. You know what I mean?'

'I understand,' I say, not quite sure where this will lead.

'No offence, but I know what most of you footballers are like.'

'None taken.'

'Therefore, Ashford, I'm giving you one chance to prove to me you are good enough for my daughter. You mess this up, and you'll be going home sooner than you think!'

'Thank you. I understand,' I say. 'I just want to say that she makes me happy. I'm not messing around. I like her.'

He gives me a stern look.

'Very well,' he says. 'Then I guess there shouldn't be any problems.'

When I go home, I feel happy and relieved. I call Aysha, who acts a bit cold at first, as I hadn't been returning her calls or messages recently. Eventually, she comes around, and I can tell she's smiling. She has no idea why her father wanted to meet and feels curious about it. Jokingly, I say that she has to try a lot harder to get it out of me.

However, my happiness is short-lived when the earlier call from Mr. V comes to mind.

15

March 23ʳᵈ

'FASCINATING… this is absolutely fascinating. What a beautiful view,' I breathe, observing the city like a gliding hawk.

The carpet of lily-white houses, with their orange Mediterranean-style rooftops, spread all over the greenness, leading towards the blue sea.

'It's the best view in Kyrenia,' admits Aysha, as we lock arms.

'The best view *of* Kyrenia,' I add, with a smile.

Since coming to Cyprus, this is my first visit to St. Hilarion Castle, and we couldn't have picked a better weekend, as this week's game is on a Monday.

The tenth-century castle, which rests high up in the Kyrenia mountain range, was built by the Byzantines and the Crusaders. At the time, the island was under risk against Arab pirates. Along with other castles like Buffavento and Kantara (also built on top of the mountains), St. Hilarion was a form of defence.

Many think the place was named after *Hilarion the Great*, an *anchorite*[13], who was active in Cyprus and Palestine in the fourth-century. However, the truth of it is that the castle was given its name after a saint, who fled to Cyprus after the Arab conquest of the Holy Land and retired here at the castle.

'Very peaceful,' breathes Aysha with a smile, thrusting her warm body against mine. I put my arm around her and hold her tight. I don't know whether it's her perfume or her natural scent that hits me, but it sure makes my heart beat faster.

I can't say who initiates the first move, but our lips lightly brush against each other. It's a perfect time and the perfect place, as we are alone above the clouds. I taste her excitement as our tongues lightly meet, and her soft, moist lips press against mine.

Unfortunately, it doesn't last long thanks to my phone ringing, ruining the moment. At first, I try to ignore it, hoping that it will stop, but it seems to get louder and more irritating. Apologetically, I dig it out from my pocket.

'Maybe it's your father,' I joke. 'He's here, hiding and spying on us!'

'Andrew!' she says, blushing and giving me a playful nudge.

'I didn't even realize you could get network from up here,' I say.

The number is withheld, and I wonder what I said about her father calling is true for a second.

---

[13] Anchorite: Someone who withdraws from secular society for religious reasons.

I answer.

'Hello Ashford,' says a smug voice. It takes me a moment to clock who it is.

'What do you want?' I ask.

'You know exactly *what* I want! And if you say anything to anyone, I swear I will hurt *them* both!'

'Hurt *who*?' I ask anxiously.

The line goes dead.

'Who was that?' asks Aysha, looking concerned.

'It's nothing to worry about,' I say dismissively.

'Didn't look that way. Look at you! You look like you've seen a ghost. You're shaking.'

She's right; I feel nauseous and a cold sweat snaking its way down my forehead.

'Andrew, who wants to hurt who?' she asks.

Eventually, I give in and tell her who it was.

'That's awful. Can't you just ignore him?' she asks.

'It's not that easy.'

'If there are opportunities to play in the Premier League, I still don't understand what you are doing out here.'

'It's not as simple as that.'

'What do you mean?' she asks, with a puzzled look. 'Why all the secrecy?'

I take in a deep breath.

'I think Lewis might be dead.'

She swallows hard. 'Dead?'

'Mr. V implied it.'

She hesitates for a moment.

'Maybe it's not true. Lewis is still down as missing, right? I mean until he's found.'

'I wouldn't put anything past Mr. V. He sounds like a sociopath.'

'So, what did he mean by saying 'hurting them both?' she asks.

Suddenly a nasty thought hits me. Could he have meant Aysha and Alp? *Maybe* he's followed me to Cyprus, which is why he's using a withheld number. He could be here at this very moment, watching us from the dark corners of the castle.

Worried, I look deep into Aysha's eyes. I just can't bear the thought of her getting hurt, or if something worse was to happen to her. I completely blame myself for putting her and her father in danger. There is only one thing to do, and that's to cool things down between us. How can I tell her that she and her father are in possible danger? I can't.

It would create unnecessary panic, which could end up getting me an early flight home.

I scan the area. All of a sudden, the ancient ruin on top of the mountains turns eerie. A peal of distant laughter comes from the bottom of the stone steps, most of which are camouflaged by overgrown weeds and wild plants. Four tourists cheerfully work their way up. I turn and look at the other end of the castle, but there is no one around.

'What is it, Andrew?' Aysha asks, worriedly.

'It's nothing,' I say, trying not to show the paranoia. 'Shall we go?' *Let's get the hell out of here*- is what I really mean.

'Good idea,' she answers. I can see she's looking concerned. *I'm freaked out* – Is what she really means.

We pace down to the car park. I look at the time, and it's three twenty-five. There is an evening training session at six, so I tell her it's best if I go home to rest. She's not overly keen on the idea, but she agrees and drives me home.

'I think I need to concentrate on the football for a while,' I say to her, as we park up.

She is silent.

'Is everything okay between us?' she asks, looking deep into my eyes, searching for an answer.

'Listen, when your father loaned me, he did so with high expectations that I'd make a substantial difference to the team. We are so close to becoming champions now. I don't want to mess things up.'

She looks out the windscreen ahead and doesn't say a word. I can sense what she's thinking: *I had to beg for my father's permission to be with you… you big bag of shit.*

I take a deep breath and rub my eyes.

'Okay, that didn't sound quite right. Here's the thing,' I say. She turns and looks at me. 'I'm in a lot of trouble. My life is in danger. At the moment, I can't be around people I love and care about.'

Whoops, did I just use the L word?

She frowns and raises a smile exposing all thirty-two of her shiny white teeth. 'Did you say love?' she asks.

'Well, just generally speaking…' I say, clearing my throat and feeling myself blush as I get out of the car.

'I guess I'll see you around.'

'Aysha, wait!' I say, leaning forward and kissing her. 'We'll meet soon, I promise. But there's something I have to take care of first.'

She sighs.

'I understand. Just don't keep me waiting too long,' she says. 'Please.'

'I'll try not to.'

She drives off.

As I make my way to the front door, it starts to rain. At the same time, I feel the vibration of my phone stubbornly ringing. Once inside, I take it out of my pocket and look to see who the caller is. I instantly recognize my mother's home number. Apart from my one, the only number I've known from memory ever since I was a child.

'Hello mum,' I say.

'Hello dear,' she answers cheerfully. 'We were just talking about you!'

'Yeah? Who with?'

'Your aunt Anita is over with her new friend, Victor. Wait, she wants to say hello…'

Anita grabs the phone out of my mother's hand, and her voice cut in.

'Hiya, stranger! How's it going?'

'Very good thanks, Anita. How're you?'

'I'm great! Can't be better, actually,' she giggles. 'I'm sure Janet mentioned that I met a handsome young fella.'

'Yes, she has. I'm happy for you,' I say as I unlock the front door and walk into the flat.

'But that's not all. You already know each other! Surprise! He says he knows you through poor Lewis. What a small world,' she says joyfully. 'In fact, he would like to talk to you!'

'Hello Andrew,' says a low husky voice, which almost makes my heart jump out my chest.

'YOU BASTARD! WHAT DO YOU WANT FROM US?' I yell.

'Easy now,' he laughs. 'Remember what we talked about earlier.'

Suddenly it dawns on me. It's not Aysha and Alp he's threatening. It's my mother and Anita.

'Didn't you check your messages? I've sent you one earlier today,' he says insolently.

Anita's voice calls out from the background, 'Check his messages? You're having a laugh!'

I vaguely remember the messenger alert tone ring earlier when I was with Aysha. I go into my inbox where an unread message flashes from Noeweir Tuhide. It reads: *You have until 17:00 Monday to come and sign the contract. Wait at Victoria train station, where someone will come and meet you. Any funny business and say goodbye to mummy and aunty. And trust me, it's easier to hurt someone when they trust you.*

'Judging by your silence, I assume the message is clear,' he says, followed by a laugh. 'I'm putting you on the loudspeaker, so you say goodbye to your mum and aunt… who may I say, is a right cougar.'

'You stay away from her!'

'Ah… ah…ah, remember where you stand, Mr. Ashford.'

I sense him heading back to the other room where my mother and aunt are happily chatting away and puts the phone onto loudspeaker.

'Say goodbye to Andy,' he says chirpily.

'Oh Andy, wish you could be here with us,' says Anita.

'So do I,' I say coldly.

'Is everything okay, dear?' asks mum, picking up on my negative vibe.

I force out a vague 'Yes,' almost choking on the word.

'Andy is just tired from all the hard training he's been doing. Hopefully, very soon he'll be back here with us!' says Mr. V.

'Yes, Victor told us a little secret... wink wink,' cuts in Anita.

'Although nothing is definite yet. Is it Andy?' Mr. V. says patronisingly.

'I gotta go,' I say, hanging up.

In a panic, I try to think and fast.

I try calling the UK police, but it won't go through. The only other person that comes to mind is Robson. Luckily this time, I get put through to him directly.

'Hello there, laddie. I'm in Edinburgh playin' a bit o' golf. How you keepin'?' he asks.

'There's an emergency! Mr. V is with my mother and aunt! He's gone to the house in Stoke!'

'What? Are you sure?'

'Yes! I spoke to him! The police need to be notified and quick!'

'So you are telling me that as we speak, this Mr. V character is at your mother's house?'

'Yes, and he's threatening to hurt them!'

'Okay, stay calm and give me the address.'

'26 Tilson Road, postcode ST1 3JZ.'

'I have a few federal connections up north. I'll get 'em to check it out!'

And that is the exact reason why I called Robson. He seems to know everyone; literally, everyone who is useful, from government officials, highly rated surgeons to police in the highest ranks.

Impatiently, I pace up and down the cramped flat, fidgeting on my phone. Every second feels like an hour, every five minutes a year. Every message, every notification, gives me a glimmer of hope, only to be short-lived. I call my mother's mobile. But she doesn't answer and eventually goes to the answerphone.

Finally, after half an hour, the phone rings. Worriedly, I glance at the withheld number and answer.

'You bloody fool! You made a big mistake!' hisses Mr. V, like an angry snake, before hanging up.

Straightaway, I call Robson, who picks up instantly.

'Andrew, I was just about to call you,' he says.

'He called me… and said… I made a big mistake! He knows that we called the police! I know he does!' I stutter hysterically.

'Now listen carefully, laddie,' Robson says, sounding calm and relaxed. 'The police raided the property. They suspect the man to be Victor Zhurov, a known gangster. Your mother and aunt were both found tied to a chair. They are okay, although your aunt has received a bit of a knock to the forehead. She's being taken to hospital for a check-up. As for Victor… he escaped just before the police turned up.'

'How did he know that they were coming?'

'Might have been luck. Probably heard sirens and acted on instinct? Either that or he has lookouts. The man's like a ghost. Always a step ahead of the police. Master of disguises too, so I'm told.'

'I need to be sure that my family will be safe.'

'Now listen here. You are still a Luton player. Therefore, the club must make sure that you and your family are safe. I will make sure your mother's home has a twenty-four-hour police surveillance.'

'Thank you.'

'And Andrew.'

'Yes?'

'You will tell me if you hear anything regarding Lewis, won't you?'

'Yes, of course.'

'Unfortunately, two months of the loan money that Doğan sent through Lewis' account never arrived. But luckily, Alp is an understanding fellow, and so we have come to an agreement.'

133

'That's good to hear.'

'Listen, if you need an agent, I can recommend a couple of good ones. You don't have to represent yourself. I believe you still have a shot at a higher-level game for next season. I really do.'

It suddenly occurs to me that I feel happy here. The island has really grown on me, and I will be sad to leave. Deep down, I know the reason why I want to stay. And the reason is Aysha.

'I'm happy here,' I answer.

'You're now your own representative. You and I will need to have a long chat at the end of the season about your future, laddie,'

'Okay,' I say, but what I'm really thinking is: *No need for a long chat, I'm staying here.*

16

'I just don't understand it dear. One minute we was chattin' nicely over a cuppa, and the next he had knocked poor Anita over the head with one of my silver candlesticks. She was out cold on the floor, you know. Thought she was dead!' mum sobs.

'Yes mum, you already told me,' I tell her. 'But try not to think about it too much!'

This is about the fifth time in the last couple of days she's told me how they were tied up in the living room. Anita, who is still in shock, isn't talking, not even to the police.

'He was being very abusive, saying how he will hurt us badly if we screamed. But then God must have heard our prayers because he suddenly disappeared, leaving us tied up. Then all these masked men broke in holding guns. Oh, it was dreadful, Andrew!'

'They were the police, mum.'

'Yes, but we didn't know that at the time. We were too shaken. I wonder why he would do such a thing to Anita? He seemed like such a nice man.'

I take a deep breath, and for a second, debate if I want to tell her too much.

'He did this to you because he wanted to hurt me and because he *wants* control over my career. I suspect he has something to do with Lewis' disappearance too.'

'Oh my goodness, Andrew!'

'We just have to wait. The police are keeping surveillance around the house, so you shouldn't worry. I am sure he'll be detained soon.'

'I'm more worried about you.'

'No need to worry,' I answer, but the truth is, I've never been so scared in my life.

After hanging up, I walk into the living room, switch on the T.V., and flick to the European News channel. Ten minutes in, I almost fall back on my chair when Lewis' face flashes on the screen. News about his disappearance is spreading fast and is now one of the top stories across Europe.

A bigger kick in the teeth comes the following morning at the local supermarket newsstand when I see my picture next to Lewis' on the front page in one of the English tabloid papers. The title asks in a thick black font:

Is Luton FC Player Guilty of the Murder of his Missing Agent, Lewis Orland?

Extreme anger and paranoia wash over me as I start feeling like a fugitive. Snatching the paper from the stand, I hurriedly scan it. I try not to make eye contact with the lady behind the counter, or the old man, walking past with a basket full of eggs.

The article is poorly written and looks somewhat rushed. It questions whether my move to Northern Cyprus is suspicious. In a nutshell, it asks why a first division footballer from England would go and play for an unrecognized team in a country out of the authority's reach? Squeezing the paper back into its slot, I hurry home.

Just as I think things cannot get any worse, they do. Jessie, my ex-fiancée, is standing at the front door. She looks pale with an expression of shame and sorrow, something that I'm not used to seeing from her. Teary-eyed, she gazes at me, as if she's been crying for a long time. She sighs a sigh of relief, throwing herself at me, giving me a tight squeeze.

'Oh Andy, I missed you, baby,' she says, caringly.

'What are you doing here?' I ask coldheartedly. 'How did you find me?'

'It wasn't exactly hard. It's a small place.'

'So, who paid for your flight?'

'What do you mean?'

'I know you don't like paying from your pocket, so who paid?'

'I did,' she answers with a frown.

'Well, I hope you bought a return ticket because I don't want you here!'

'Don't be like that,' she begs. 'Okay, I messed up. I made a mistake. Is this how much I'm worth to you?'

'Worth?' I grunt.

'Please, can I come in?' she asks.

'I tell you what you can do. You can get lost!' I exclaim.

'He hit me, Andrew! Pablo beat me! You always said that you were against violence towards women, so at least have some bloody sympathy!'

'Sympathy?' I chuckle. 'While I was in the hospital, having an operation, he was screwing you, in *our* bed!'

Pausing for a moment, she shuts her eyes and runs a hand through her hair. What she always did to keep her temper under control- kind of self-defence, or a calming mechanism- not that it ever worked.

'Look, Andy baby, give me one more chance, and I promise… I promise I'll make it up to you, okay?' she says softly under her breath, almost singing the words.

I take my phone out and type her and Pablo's names into Google, bringing up all the pictures of them taken by the paparazzi, plus one or two articles by a couple of cheap gossip magazines, and then push the screen right up to her face.

'You dated him for four months, and then he got a transfer back to Spain… probably because he couldn't wait to get away. You scared him off… and now you come running back to me?'

'It's not like that?'

'I know exactly what it's like,' I say, taking my wallet out from my pocket and pulling out some notes. 'Here's three hundred quid. Should be enough for your flight home.'

'Andrew?' she says, shocked, but eyeing the cash.

'And let me help you a bit more,' I say dialling a number for a taxi. 'I will even get you a ride to the airport!'

'But that's not fair! I just got here,' she says, with the three hundred pounds, all in fifties now in her hand. 'At least let me have a cup of tea. Or even a glass of water.'

Feeling incredibly uncomfortable, I stay silent. I just can't deal with this right now. The taxi driver says that it will take him a good ten minutes to come, so I tell her she has enough time to use the bathroom and quickly have a glass of water.

Like a curious cat, she strolls in, looking around.

'A lot different than your last place,' she mutters.

'My last place was in London.'

She mumbles something under her breath, which I don't quite make out, but it doesn't matter, as I am not interested in what she has to say. Nor am I interested in making conversation with her.

'The toilet is at the end of the corridor. Last door on the left,' I say.

She thanks me and goes in.

'Are you sure you don't want to come back to London with me?' her voice echoes from inside the bathroom.

'That's a joke, right?' I answer, sourly.

'Only if you want it to be,' she replies.

I rush into the kitchen and pour her a glass of water from the fridge-tap.

The quicker she drinks it, the faster she can leave, as long as the taxi gets here on time. After five minutes, she is still in the toilet as I stand at the end of the corridor, glass of water in hand. A car horn beeps outside. *At last!*

'Your taxi is here!' I call.

The toilet flushes, and she spends another three minutes thoroughly washing her hands. If I know her as well as I think I do, she's also renewing her makeup.

Gradually, the bathroom door unlocks and swings open. Before she walks out, a strong scent of perfume fills the corridor, making me gag. She walks up and stands in front of me with a seductive smile. I pass her the glass of water.

'Taxi!' I say bluntly.

I follow her downstairs to make sure she leaves, which turns out to be a big mistake.

'At least you got me a nice ride,' she says, walking up to the taxi, dragging her large suitcase along.

Almost all the taxis in Cyprus are Mercedes. Ali Fırat, the driver I called, jumps out to give her a hand to place her designer-brand beast of a suitcase into the boot.

Being one of the more reliable drivers, I use Ali going out certain nights when I know that I'll be drinking.

'Alo Mr. Andrew,' he says, with his eyes locked on Jessie, who looks out of place at this time of the morning with her shiny silver mini skirt, red high-heeled shoes, and large cream-coloured furry coat. I can tell what he is thinking and I don't blame him for doing so.

'Hello, Ali. Make sure she gets to Ercan Airport and catches a flight home,' I say.

'No worry,' he smiles, forcing down the boot.

'You be careful with that luggage now, it's very expensive,' says Jessie.

She then turns and gives me another hug.

'I'm going to miss you, baby,' she says, tightly locking her lips onto mine.

I try hard to set myself free, convinced I heard the clicking of a camera. A car then skids past, leaving a smell of burnt rubber. I pray no one was around to see Jessie kissing me. Cyprus is a small place, so gossip spreads fast.

Giving me an evil smile and a wink, she places herself in the backseat and patronisingly waves with each of her thin fingers wiggling like worms.

As the taxi disappears around the corner, it hits me that someone could have taken a picture of her kissing me. Maybe it wasn't a car speeding past at all. Perhaps it was a photographer getting away. Or even worse, perhaps this was a set up to capture photos of her and me together.

The more I think about it the more likely it sounds, as Jessie would definitely not pay for a flight here.

In a panic, I give her a call, but she doesn't answer. I then call Ali Fırat and ask to talk to her.

'But Mr. Andrew,' he stutters, 'A car stop in front! It was her friend and they go to airport together!'

'What? You're bloody joking!' I cry in disbelief.

'It was the man who was taking your pictures,' he adds.

'My pictures? I'm not following you.'

'Yes, he was in the car taking pictures of you and her,'

Great! I fell right into the trap. The photographer must have come with Jessie. Soon, I can expect a call from Mr. V, threatening to send the pictures to the press, or even worse, directly to Alp or Aysha.

* * *

There's no way I'm going to let this go, so I jump into my car and speed towards Ercan Airport, hoping to catch them on the way. Unfortunately, they are too far ahead and I end up driving to the airport through the flood-ridden roads in the torrential rain. I look everywhere- and I mean everywhere- from the check-in queues to the cafes. They couldn't have already checked-in, not with these queues. And the next flight isn't for another three hours.

I try calling Jessie again and this time, she answers.

'You bitch! Where are you… and your photographer friend?'

'Wow, we have got some brains, haven't we? Never thought you'd work it out,' she giggles.

'Why did you do it?'

'Why do you think? Money!'

'That's enough,' echoes a man's voice in the background, with an Eastern European accent- the photographer.

'Where the hell are you?' I ask, just as an announcement about a delayed flight, echoes from above.

She laughs an evil laugh. 'Oh baby, you poor thing. You went all the way to Ercan Airport. But we are on our way to Larnaca,' she says mockingly.

'Right! That's enough,' repeats the man.

'Who put you up to this?' I ask.

But the line goes dead.

17

SINCE Jessie's disturbing visit, I had little sleep and hoped no one had seen us together, but unfortunately, that wasn't the case. When it was my turn to give Peter a lift to training yesterday, he was quieter than usual. As we arrived at the training ground, he shook his head in disapproval and told me that he saw Jessie and me kissing from his window. I tried my best to explain that she turned up out of the blue, and the kiss was against my will, but I don't think he bought it.

'You are playing with fire, bro!' he warned. 'I told you before that dating Aysha is a *big* responsibility. You mess this up and your job's on the line. And guess what? You seem to be doing everything you can *to* mess it up!'

'I'm not! Trouble keeps following me!' I told him. 'Did you see anyone else there?'

'There was a taxi driver.'

'How about a man taking pictures of us?'

'What? Are you mad? Are you out of your mind? You were being photographed?'

'Apparently so. Did you see what the man looked like? Or what kind of car he was driving? Anything like that?'

'No! I was too shocked looking at you locking lips! I only looked out to see what all the noise was. She had a mouth on her!'

'Yep, she does. Likes to be heard.'

On the way back after training, Peter had given me another lecture on how I'd put my career in danger. I didn't bother answering, so he got the message and kept quiet after that, but promised me that he wouldn't tell anyone about what he had seen. Two days have passed since with no mention of the subject.

Today I try to stay focused on the game against Gönyeli. Training has been hard. I feel physically ready, but I'm not so sure how I feel mentally.

Gönyeli is a small town just north of Nicosia. Their football club has been flying high in the Northern Cyprus Super League in the previous years. However, this year just hasn't been their season. The manager started blaming the club for the lack of transfers- the ones they had already made were substandard- then he resigned a couple of weeks ago. The team is now mid-table and looks like they will remain there until the end of the season.

As the team bus works its way to the Ali Naci Karacan Stadı, I notice quite a lot of development in a town that offers mostly farming. The stadium that holds around five thousand fans, was named after *Ali Naci Karacan*, a Turkish journalist, who founded the well-known *Milliyet* newspaper.

144

The match will be played at the same time as the Çetinkaya and Lefke game. If Çetinkaya loses or draws, and we get a win against Gönyeli, we go on top of the table.

The bus pulls up at the rear carpark, with the roaring from inside the stadium at full blast. The chants, combined with the drums, bells and horns echo wildly, sending a clear message: *We've put on a show for you, now you put on a show for us!*

'This will be a game! Our supporters are equal to theirs for once,' says Ahmet, who followed the team bus and parked right next to it.

Sporting our white away-shirts and navy-blue shorts, we walk onto a hostile field alongside our opponents, who are in all red and are looking to grab three points off a high-flying team. And boy don't they let us know about it! After winning the toss and kicking off, straight away they come at us with all guns blazing.

Only two minutes in, Adil is too slow and brings down their nippy striker.

The ref blows for a foul and shows him a yellow card.

'Oh, come on ref! Exaggerated fall!' he cries.

Not answering, the referee indicates for him to stand back.

'It's a bit early for a card,' says Hakan.

'You want one too?' the ref snaps.

This will be a tougher game than anticipated. In general, the referees have been okay, but there have certainly been a couple of biased ones, and unfortunately, today's one fits that list.

In the twenty-second minute, Hakan gives a superb pass to Ünal, as I get into space just on the edge of the penalty area, without falling into the offside trap. Ünal passes the ball towards me, but it gets deflected off a defender and falls behind. Still, I manage to control it, dribble past the first defender, then the second, who tries a sliding-tackle, missing my ankle by inches.

I remember what Mr. Reynolds, the youth academy goalkeeping coach, used to tell his keepers. *Never stand too far from the goal, even when there's a defender present.* Obviously, this keeper isn't familiar with that rule and runs out like a mad man.

This is too easy. I think to myself.

I chip the ball over him and the defender, into the goal.

The fans go wild. Adrenalin rushes through my veins as I sprint towards them to celebrate with my teammates following.

I come face to face with Alp, who is further up the stands, clapping and satisfied. Next to him sits Aysha, with her large Gucci sunglasses covering most of her face. She smiles proudly. Ever since the terrifying incident involving my mother and aunt, she has been incredibly supportive.

Maybe it's how she acted in the car after St. Hilarion; the way we left things hanging in the air. She admitted she was selfish and, at the time failed to see how dangerous the situation was. I'm surprised she came to this game, as she

146

hardly ever goes to the away games. Deep inside, I hope the reason she came is to watch me, and not just because the team is on the verge of winning the title.

'Okay! That's enough celebrating! Back to your places!' calls Remzi from the other side of the pitch.

This time Gönyeli is better organised and composes a threatening attack.

Luckily a shot deflects off Peter and ends up in the hands of Süleyman, our goalkeeper.

Oktay, the midfielder who is a bank manager of some bank on the outskirts of Kyrenia, receives the goal kick. He looks up at the wings, hesitates, and then runs forward a few paces, before passing it high towards me.

'USE THE WINGS!' cries Remzi with frustration, chucking a water bottle onto the ground.

Stopping the ball with my chest, I turn and try something I haven't done since after the operation. I accelerate, fast, skipping past three players until I'm one on one with the keeper. This time he doesn't commit and waits for the shot. Looking right, I shoot left. He doesn't move and just stands there, blaming the defenders for the goal.

A couple of years back, while having a pint down the local pub, a friend once asked me about the player differences between the professional, semi-professional, and amateur football leagues. I gave him three answers: discipline, fitness, and of course, the paycheque. Not that I like to brag, but leading up to both the goals today, the first two points were unquestionably valid.

Our fans roar with excitement, while the opposing ones boo and hiss, at their team.

As I run back to the field, I feel a sudden sharp pain to the scar, where my leg was operated. Maybe the sprint before the goal was not such a good idea. I look at the scoreboard. There are still fifteen minutes remaining until half time. I walk around trying to shake it off. Whenever the ball comes to me, I just pass it on. Luckily, as we are two up, Remzi wants to secure the score and not commit as much.

Suddenly our fans cheer and start to celebrate. In confusion, I turn and look at Ünal, who has a broad grin across his face.

'What's happening?' I ask.

'Lefke just scored in the other game!' he replies. 'If the scores remain like this, we'll be leaders!'

Come half time, I have no choice but to tell Remzi about the ongoing pain in my leg. For the remainder of the match, I watch from the subs bench. The final score is three-two, and another three points are in the bag. The Çetinkaya- Lefke game finishes a one-all draw, which is enough to see us go on the top of the table.

As for the pain in my leg, an MRI scan the following day concludes a pulled muscle with no ligamental damage. I live to fight another day.

❉ ❉ ❉

'It's your call,' she says, smiling. 'What do you fancy?'

I give her a look and reply, 'Something I haven't had since leaving England.'

'Really? What's that?'

'It's the most popular dish in the UK,' I say, giving her a clue.

'Yes, I got it! There's a place that serves brilliant fish 'n chips! They even serve mushy peas on the-'

'Curry!' I cut in, laughing. 'I miss a nice hot curry!'

'Oh, I see,' she chuckles. 'I know just the place.'

I've seen a couple of curry houses scattered around Kyrenia, but never had the chance to eat in any of them. Or maybe I prefer to go on recommendation, and as funny as it sounds, I take my Indian food seriously.

'What's the place called?' I ask.

'It's called Jashan's. It's in Karaoğlanoğlu[14].'

After a ten minutes' drive, we pull into a carpark of an authentic Indian restaurant with a red and yellow building. A couple of friendly waiters greet us upon entering. On the left is a bar facing the dining area, with Indian music blasting through the speakers in the corners of the room. We are shown to our table by one of the waiters, who hands us the menus.

As we order our drinks, a man walks past with his eyes locked on me. I try to ignore him, but it isn't possible. He approaches our table with a look of surprise on his face.

'Wow! Look, babe, it's Ashford. I can't believe it's you!' he says, looking at me with surprise.

---

[14] Karaoğlanoğlu: A town west of Kyrenia.

149

His wife (or partner) scrutinises me carefully, trying to recognize the celebrity.

I just smile and say, 'Hi.'

He looks like a stereotypical football fan, with a shaved head, a collection of tattoos on both arms and is wearing the old Barcelona Football Club jersey.

'Mate! I'm a diehard Luton FC fan,' he says with a proud grin.

'That's right. He is!' agrees his wife.

'Look!' he adds, showing me the fading tattoo of the club's logo, above his left wrist.

'Very nice,' I say.

'So, the rumours are true then. You're playin' for a team here!'

'That's right. I am,' I answer.

Amused, Aysha smiles at me, trying not to burst out laughing.

'I read somewhere before that you was headed to the Premier League,' he says with a slight frown.

'I had a long-term injury,' I remind him.

'Oh yeah, I forgot about that,' he says.

'Do you mind?' he asks, handing his wife his mobile so that she can take a picture.

'Not at all,' I say, getting up.

Standing next to him, I force a smile as the phone flashes a couple of times, taking our pictures.

'I recommend the chicken korma,' he says. 'It's brilliant!'

'Thanks, I'll bear that in mind,' I say as they walk away.

'So, that's one chicken korma for you,' says Aysha with a smile.

'I'll have a Chicken madras!' I answer, sitting back down.

My phone rings. It's a withheld number.

'No number. Your dad is probably checking on us again,' I joke, but also feel anxious that it might be Mr. V.

'I wouldn't put it past him,' she laughs.

I answer. To my surprise, it's Cliff Robson.

'Ashford, we need to talk,' he says.

The tone in his voice sends shivers down my spine, with several thoughts flashing through my mind. Is it regarding Lewis? Has he been found? And if so, is he alive or dead? Or is it something to do with Mr. V?

Whatever the reason, it is incredibly unusual for Robson to call directly, not to mention this late on in the evening.

Excusing myself from Aysha, I walk through the variety of curry aromas coming from the plates and pots from the other tables and out into the car park where it's silent, with no distractions.

'Okay, I'm alone,' I tell Robson, hearing my stomach loudly growling with hunger.

'Right laddie, there's no easy way of saying this,' he says. 'I just want you to know that what I'm about to tell you, was not purely my decision. It's just been one bad publicity after another, which doesn't do the club's reputation any favours. Even the stocks have fallen after the accusations linking you to Lewis' disappearance. A board members' meeting was held and a decision has been reached. I'm sorry to say that your

151

contract has been terminated. We are parting ways with immediate effect.'

There's an uncomfortable silence as I try and digest the information.

'Hang on. You don't think I have something to do with Lewis' disappearance?' I say.

'As I told you, it's not in my hands anymore. The club is suffering.'

'So that's it then,' I reply.

'I'm sorry, laddie,' he says sympathetically. 'My advice to you would be to stay there for a while until things here blow over. Things are a bit unsettled at the moment.'

'The funny thing is Cliff, is that it was both yours and Lewis' idea for me to come here!'

'I'm sorry,' he repeats. 'There is nought I can do. You come out here anytime soon, and they will crucify you.'

'Well, that was easy, wasn't it?'

'Goodbye, laddie,' he says.

The phone goes dead.

I stand in the dark carpark for a few moments, looking at the ground, feeling lost, trying to make out my own feet, and wishing I could disappear into the darkness. For the first time in my life, I feel the freedom of becoming a free agent and not belonging to any club. Although it shouldn't bother me- as staying out here with Aysha seems a dream come true- but being labelled a suspected murderer, is genuinely frightening. I don't blame the board for axing me; I mean, who in their right mind wants an agent-murdering fugitive in their team?

Robson, on the other hand, can go to hell. I head back to the restaurant, with a loss of appetite, thanks to the cut-throat call.

'I've ordered your madras,' says Aysha, when I'm back inside.

She notices me looking pale.

'What's wrong?' she asks.

'That was Cliff Robson, the Luton FC chairman. My contract has been terminated.' I tell her.

'Sorry to hear that.'

'So am I.'

'How come?'

I'm quiet for a moment.

'To cut a long story short, the media are blaming me for Lewis' disappearance... murder. So, the board committee is protecting the club's best interest.'

She puts her hand over mine, giving me a sympathetic look, as the waiter delicately pours rosé into her glass, before moving onto mine. If it were any other evening, everything would have been perfect, but unfortunately, it isn't. I decide that I will go and talk to Alp tomorrow about my future with Doğan.

Not wanting to ruin the evening further, I won't mention anything else to Aysha about football. I'm happy just talking to her about her favourite films instead.

18

WE drive towards the old harbour past the Rocks Hotel's glittering lights, followed by the Dome Hotel, which is not as glamorous but is the oldest and therefore the most established in Kyrenia. For some, the *most established* part would be debatable. But one thing that cannot be argued against is its perfect location next to the sea, half a kilometre away from the old harbour.

Kyrenia is a peaceful Mediterranean city, with minimal noise pollution compared to other cities, and boasts a low crime rate. As a whole, Northern Cyprus is a safe place. It offers a good standard of living. Anyone who tells you that it is an Islamic country with strict religious rules couldn't be more wrong.

Young couples hold hands, strolling the streets, towards the harbour. As elsewhere, a group of girls, some wearing miniskirts, with their hair freshly made for the Friday night entertainment, joyfully make their way to local bars. At the same time, other people sit in small cafes and the micro-pubs in the harbour, drinking cocktails and pints of beer. And yet the call for prayer can be heard echoing in the background. A topic I decide to question Aysha about.

'Being an Islamic country, how come this place is so relaxed about religion?' I ask.

Taken aback with the unusual question, she asks, 'Why wouldn't it be? The politics do not run on religion and sharia law certainly doesn't exist here.'

'Neither does it exist in Turkey. But having said that, the Turkish Cypriots seem more relaxed when it comes to religion,' I say.

'On a couple of occasions when I was small, I joined my grandma in fasting, but I never went to the mosque. No one here imposes their beliefs onto others.'

'But as I pass by, I sometimes see many people outside the mosque on Fridays,' I challenge her.

'I'd say ninety percent of them are from the mainland,' she answers as we pass by the harbour's entrance and head away towards the city centre. 'There are a lot of people from Pakistan living and working here too. They are committed to their religion, and they certainly go to the mosque on Fridays.'

'Yes, that's true.'

'How about you? You're a Christian, right?' she asks, staring at the shop windows on the narrow high street as we slowly drive past.

'I come from a protestant family, but I'm agnostic.'

'In a way, you are like me. You believe in God, but not religion.'

'I believe there is a strong power. But religion was created by man thousands of years ago for civilization purposes.' I explain.

'That's an interesting way of putting it.'

'Plus, unfortunately, there is one dominant religion in the world nowadays,' I add.

She gives me an odd look and asks, 'Which one's that?'

'Money!'

She smiles.

'But it's true. Isn't it?'

She thinks for a couple of seconds and replies, 'Yeah, I suppose it is.'

We don't say much after that. In fact, we don't talk at all.

The silence takes me back to the earlier conversation I had with Robson. I feel frustration and anger the way the media and he has treated me, leaving me in limbo to face my forsaken destiny. Occasionally there is the odd coverage on the news about a failed footballer living on the streets and sleeping in shelters. Or others who are treated in rehab for certain reasons, be it alcoholism or drugs. Their situations must be worse than what I'm going through- a lot worse.

At least financially, things aren't too bad, thanks to a healthy bank account, and as long as I can agree to terms with Doğan, I'll be happy to ride out another season out here.

However much I try and comfort myself, it's indubitable that things have been tough always watching over my shoulder since the beginning of the season. It's true when they say that you can't plan your future. If it wasn't for Lewis' gambling or the long-term injury, I know for sure that I would still be playing for Luton FC and pushing hard to break into the Premier League. I ask myself if I would be as happy as I am now. I take a look outside at the calmness of Kyrenia, and then at Aysha, and think to myself, *definitely not.*

'Are you okay?' she asks. 'You've gone quiet.'

I look at her and smile, 'I'm good.'

'You're still upset about the call from Robson.'

'Everything will be okay,' I answer.

The Focus pulls up next to her mountain of a Range Rover she had left beneath my apartment block.

'It's not that late yet if you want to come upstairs for a coffee,' I offer.

'Maybe a quick coffee,' she replies, checking the time.

'Really? I thought that maybe we could also watch a movie on *Flicks.* There are a couple of new releases that are meant to be quite good.'

She contemplates it for a moment and then says, 'A movie, huh? All right, why not.'

We take the lift up to my flat. She's surprised when I tell her that this is the first time I'm using the lift and prefer to take the stairs instead. Although she tells me I'm crazy for never using the lift, I sense that she thinks it's cute in her own - *flirtatious, fallen in love, therefore, I can't do any wrong*- type of way.

'Can I ask why?' she chuckles.

'Because it's good exercise and I just don't trust this lift. I heard that someone got stuck in here for two hours once.'

'No way! Well, I suppose it wouldn't be *that* bad if we both got stuck in it *together.*'

I stop searching for the house keys and look into her eyes for a second, then, hesitating, I continue searching for them again. She reaches out and places both her hands over my trouser pockets, giving them a light stroke.

'They're not there,' she whispers.

Some things just happen spontaneously. I Lean down and kiss her, taking in the scent of spearmint and wine, as our tongues meet.

After a good two minutes of multi-tasking, I locate the house key in my blazer's left inner pocket. Once inside, we continue from where we left off until we somehow find ourselves at the doorway of the kitchen. She says that she'll make the coffees, giving me a final peck on the lips, turning on the lights, and heading inside.

'If you're hoping for Turkish coffee, you're in for a disappointment,' I say, clearing my throat.

'No Turkish coffee? Nescafe it is then.'

'Unless you prefer filter.'

'Filter coffee is better. I see you have a machine in here.'

'Yes, I do. It's a healthier choice. Do you know how to work it?'

'Umm… on second thoughts, it's best if you make them,' she says.

'Did it come with the flat?'

'No, I bought it.'

I follow her into the kitchen and head over to the cupboard.

'So, do you have any films in mind?' I ask her as I open the cupboard and take out the filter coffee packet.

'Anything new I'm okay with,' she answers.

'So, no classics then,' I say, dropping two spoonful of ground filter coffee into the machine and pressing the start button.

'Not tonight. Unless you want me to fall asleep,' she says, picking up a damp cloth near the basin and wiping the spilled coffee granules from the counter. I get the feeling that she isn't joking. She looks worn and tired, probably the after-effects of the wine.

'Thank you, but you don't need to clean up,' I say, as the machine begins to hiss and release drops of filtered-coffee into its jug at a steady pace.

When the coffee is ready, mugs in hand, we head into the living room. Curling up like a kitten and looking extremely cosy, she makes herself comfy on the sofa in front of the T.V., I place myself next to her and grab the remote.

'Let's look at the *recently added* list,' I say.

'That one looks interesting,' she states, taking a sip of coffee. *Really?* I think to myself. *Does she really want to watch a romance between a middle-aged couple in the Irish countryside?*

I remember she told me once that she loves romance novels, so the movies probably go hand in hand. All her favourite films that she has ever talked about are love films- *Titanic, The Notebook, Romeo and Juliet. But seriously, if this movie doesn't make her go to sleep, I don't know what will!* I prefer thrillers myself. Anyway, if she wants a romance, she will have a romance!

'Why not,' I say.

As long as she is next to me, I don't care what we watch. At this moment in time, I need the company. I feel vulnerable and I cannot bear the thought of being alone. Not tonight, not now.

Leaning forward, she places her cup on the table. I subtly move my hand closer to hers. She also does the same until they both meet halfway, and tightly lock together. Her breathing gets heavier and more intense as our lips press together. I gently slide my hand down her back, feeling her warm and soft skin. The blue light reflecting from the television screen is the only source of light lighting up the darkroom. Slowly she starts to undo her shirt buttons, making my heart race even faster. She then removes her shirt, exposing her bra, puts her arms around my neck, and presses her firm breasts against my chest as we continue to kiss.

I get a vibe I shouldn't go any further and in no way does she encourage it either. It's like a clear message: *No sex before marriage!* - A message that would usually scare me away, but for some reason, this time it doesn't, and it only makes me feel satisfied. It can wait, as I have the utmost respect for Hasan Alp, and don't want to upset him in any way.

My phone buzzes and pings as a picture comes in via messenger, sent by a name I dread- a name that has become my daily nightmare- NOEWEIR TUHIDE.

'Who's messaging you this late?' Aysha asks, jokingly, but I can tell she is quite curious.

'It's nobody important,' I say as I open the image file, holding the phone at an angle, so it's out of her vision.

It takes a couple of seconds to register what I am looking at, and when I do, I almost drop the phone. Hurriedly, I shut it, placing it in my pocket.

The bastard was behind Jessie's visit. He'd organised the photoshoot, and now he's sent me a sample!

I ask myself *why* he would go to such extreme lengths to be my agent. Okay, in the past there has been interest from Premier League clubs, but realistically I'm not a star player that someone would go this far into blackmailing just to become my agent. It just doesn't make sense. There's a piece missing in the puzzle.

'You're in deep thought again, Andrew. If this doesn't cheer you up, I don't know what will!' says Aysha, looking concerned.

'No, it's nothing. I'm happy you're here. It's just that-'

'Look, all you need to do is talk to my dad. I'm sure you can come to some agreement,' she explains and then pauses. 'It's the message, isn't it?' she asks coldly. 'Who is it from?'

'No one you know,' I say.

She sighs.

'I'm here, Andrew. Talk to me!'

'It's getting late,' I say.

She gets up and retrieves her jacket from the chair next to the table.

'You're right. It's *getting* late,' she utters.

I take a deep breath, realizing my mistake.

'I didn't mean it like that,' I say, apologetically.

She puts on her jacket and heads for the front door.

'Aysha, what I meant is, I just want us to relax. I don't want to discuss my life or my career at this time of the night.'

'I think I need to go. Don't take this the wrong way, but you need to be alone with your thoughts.'

'Stay,' I beg.

She shakes her head, 'It's getting late. I'm tired.'

'We're okay though, right?'

She stops and answers 'Right.'

With a swift '*Bye*,' she leaves. Not even a kiss. The time is half-past midnight. I stare at the photo sent by Mr. V and debate whether I should write back, but I decide not to retaliate, as that's just what he wants.

Instead, I ignore the message altogether. Jessie is a real pro at doing what she does. She has her arms passionately around me, giving me a kiss that seems deceptively meaningful. It makes me look as if I enjoyed every second of it.

I decide that I must tell Aysha before any more of these pictures are exposed or even worse, reach the press.

19

THE following day I force myself out of bed, feeling super drained. The time is half ten. Great! I've overslept! But that's not surprising, considering I couldn't bring myself to sleep until the early hours of the morning. I dared not look at the time, especially when I noticed the light creeping through the curtains. The slightest sound had irritated me and kept me from dozing off. I was awake all night, thinking.

Outside, a dog barks loudly at a passing car.

'Shut up!' I say, massaging my temples with the tips of my fingers, hoping that it will relieve the headache. But unfortunately, it doesn't.

After a quick shower, I brush my teeth, throw on a tracksuit, and walk into the kitchen. I'm pleased there's still some filter coffee in the jug, leftover from last night. I press the heat button and grab a darkening banana from the basket, which surprisingly doesn't taste too bad. I then gulp down two Paracetamols with the lukewarm coffee.

Looking outside the kitchen window reminds me of why I've fallen in love with this place. Like most days of the year, the sun is shining. There's only one cloud in the sky- a single sheet cutting through the Beşparmak mountain range- surrounding St. Hilarion Castle. I feel like taking another trip up there to sit on a rock and observe the city from above. But this morning, I have to meet Alp. I've reached another crossroads in my life.

As I walk down the stairs, I bump into Peter.

'What's up, Pete?'

'How're you doing?' he says, removing his headphones.

'Good. Yourself?'

'All right.'

'Just on my way to see Alp.'

'I see his daughter was here last night.'

'Is there anything you don't know? You're like a walking CCTV camera!'

'Need to make sure the neighbourhood's safe,' he says, music blaring out of his headphones, which dangle down his neck.

'Wait! Did you say you're on your way to see Alp?'

'Yes.'

'I think he's got a meeting in Nicosia this morning. Check with Ahmet first, though.'

'Okay, will do.'

'And Andrew-'

'Yeah?'

'I'm sorry to hear about the accusations going around, linking you to your Lewis' disappearance. Just want you to know that the team's behind you,' he says sympathetically.

So, everyone knows. News spreads fast.

164

'Thanks, I appreciate the support.' I say. 'Luton have terminated my contract, by the way.'

'I'm sorry to hear that,' he sighs.

Taking Peter's advice, I call Ahmet first, who confirms Alp is indeed in Nicosia and expected to be in his office at two.

Then I give Aysha a call, but she's busy with work. She says she'll call back later.

Trying to kill time, I drive around aimlessly. In a moment of madness, I stop at the hard shoulder and start typing her a message.

Need to talk to you. It's urgent, but then I delete it. The incident with Jessie is eating me alive. If I'm going to tell Aysha, I need to man up and tell her face to face.

I drive to Alsancak Park, a place I passed by a dozen times, but never actually checked out. It's meant to be one of the locals' favourites for outdoor walking. Aysha had once mentioned the path is two kilometres and takes about twenty minutes to circle. Two separate lanes run side by side, disappearing into the forest of pine trees.

Taking in the unblemished fresh air and the comforting sweet smell of pine trees, I follow the paths. I get tempted to run when a couple of joggers pass me by but remember that I need to save my energy for the afternoon training session, so I walk briskly instead.

A man dressed in white, with greying hair, runs past, heavily panting. He seems fit for his age of fifty-something. He slows down next to me.

'Right there?' he says in a cockney accent.

'Hi,' I reply.

'How're you finding it here?'

Looking around at the trees and the crisp blue winter sky, I answer, 'Nice place.'

'No, not the park!' he laughs. 'I mean Northern Cyprus!'

'I've settled in quite well.'

'Good to hear.'

He looks around and is now walking closer to me.

'I suppose you haven't got much choice, have you?'

'Not at the moment,' I say dismissively.

I walk faster, hoping he'll get the message I'm not looking for company. But he doesn't and keeps up.

'I was hoping to bump into you.'

I look at him blankly.

'Really? Why's that?' I ask, confused, hoping he's not some nutcase.

'We are in the same boat if you see what I mean. Except, mine's for major VAT fraud,' he winks, tapping his nose with his index finger and looking profoundly proud. 'You still have to be careful though. According to some sources, the police here have started working closely with the police in the UK. Not to mention that the Northern Cyprus government has offered to sign an extradition treaty with the UK. Luckily, it's been refused, as the British government doesn't have diplomatic relations with the north. But still… the likes of us aren't wanted here.'

For a moment, I try to digest the information. When I do, I get irritated that a fraudster would have the audacity to compare himself with me.

'I'm nothing like you! You piece of shit!' I snap.

He stops and winces. I hear his heavy breathing fading the further away I pace. A crow screeches from the top of one of the trees, and a baby's cry echoes from the playground behind. I feel his eyes locked on me. I don't break my stride and try to stay strong, not showing how terrified I am. After all, he is a fugitive, and heaven knows what he is capable of. Looking at the situation logically, I'd guess he wouldn't try anything, as needs to maintain his low profile.

'ONCE YOU'VE BEEN LABELLED, THERE'S NO ESCAPE! BUT THE PARANOIA... IT WILL EAT YOU ALIVE!' he calls.

I continue walking at a fast pace, trying to block out his words.

Have I really been labelled a fugitive? Frustration runs through my entire body. I decide to run and relieve stress. I complete one round in less than fifteen minutes. So I run another. I don't see him in the second round. Undoubtedly like a ghost, he's disappeared into the woods, watching from the dark corners.

I go back to the car, get inside and do something I haven't done in a very long time, something that has been building up inside me over the last couple of weeks. I begin to cry.

Firmly I knock on the door.

'Come in!' calls Alp from inside his office.

He stands up and walks over, kissing me on both cheeks, which I used to find awkward when I first arrived, but now I'm slowly getting used to this eastern tradition. To be honest, it's not so much a kiss, but a contact of the cheeks while shaking hands. Nevertheless, I feel honoured, as it's the first one I've received from Alp, which probably means he's accepted me into his family.

'How was the curry last night?' he asks, signalling for me to take a seat.

'It was good,' I say. 'But it would've been more enjoyable if it wasn't for Cliff Robson's call.'

'Really? He called you in person?'

'He did.'

'What did he want?'

'My contract with Luton has been terminated.'

'Sorry to hear that,' he says, slowly placing himself on his chair. 'So that's the reason why Luton called while I was out this morning. The club secretary took the call. I was just about to call them back.'

'So, what will happen now? Where do I stand with Doğan?' I ask.

He picks up a silver pen and scribbles on a large pad resting on his desk in front of him.

'You're having a good season and already top scorer in the league. What's more, the team is on top form and looks likely champions. Therefore, I don't want to unbalance things. The remainder of the loan that was to be paid to Luton will be paid directly to you instead.'

I feel myself smile- probably the first one of the day.

'And if you decide to stay another year, it can be arranged. But I can't guarantee the payment will be as high,' he says apologetically.

'I understand,' I say, knowing that the pay is already exceptionally high for a team that isn't supported by FIFA.

'You'd better make sure we are champions this year, or I might reconsider,' he says jokingly. However, I feel an element of seriousness in his tone.

I thank him and as I'm leaving, he stops me and says, 'Ashford, why don't you come over for dinner soon. My wife is dying to meet you. She's one hell of a cook!'

'Thank you. That's very kind of you,' I say.

Shortly after exiting the club building, I receive a call from Aysha. I tell her about the meeting with her father. She's happy to hear the outcome but still tired and stressed with work. Not the best day to tell her about the visit from Jessie. Maybe that's what Mr. V is hoping for- that I shoot myself in the foot by telling her. I cannot give him that satisfaction. I cannot let him win!

※ ※ ※

It's been half an hour since training finished, which involved rather apathetic passing and shooting practices, followed by a short half-hearted game amongst ourselves. Maybe it bears no differences to the previous training sessions, and if not, it's just the way I feel today. My lack of energy has dragged me down so deep that I'm nearing a black hole where everything is dark and glum; even the food I eat is tasteless. I get out of the shower and start drying when the doorbell rings, followed by a loud knock. Hurriedly, I throw on some clothes and rush to answer it. I contemplate whether it's Aysha, but she usually calls before coming, plus she wouldn't knock so hard as if trying to bring down the door.

'Who's it?'

'Mustafa Hamza,' grunts Hamza's voice.

I open the door. I'm not surprised to see him. Suddenly I start to panic when I remember what the man in the park had told about the police here working with the police in England to capture fugitives who are hiding on the island.

'How can I help you?' I ask.

'Can I come in?' he says, raising a forceful smile.

I show him into the living room where he makes himself comfortable on a chair, examining the surroundings.

'Something tells me this isn't a social visit,' I say.

'That is correct. It is not.'

'So how can I help you?' I ask, my heart racing faster.

'There's one gang member remaining in jail from the night you were kidnapped.'

'Nice. And what happened to the others?' I ask.

'They were bailed out. Only the driver remains.'

'Bailed out?'

'They only served three weeks. I have no other information for you,' he says, coldly. 'But the driver isn't going anywhere for a while.'

'They only got three weeks?'

'Let's just say there was a lack of evidence against them. The driver, however, was the scapegoat.'

'So… why are you telling me this?' I ask.

'I can arrange for you to meet him.'

Confused, I look at Hamza; his grey eyes barely blink.

'Maybe you can try and get some information regarding Lewis,' he adds.

'Ok-ay… so what's in it for you?'

'Nothing.'

'Then why are you trying to help me?'

'I'm doing it as a favour.'

'As a favour to whom?'

'Ahmet, my cousin.'

'Wait… you're Ahmet's cousin?'

'Correct. Every passing day Lewis is missing is a danger for *you*. At the moment, the media is pointing fingers. Next, it will be the police! The driver might have information that saves your career and reputation. Your club has already washed their hands with you. You are now Doğan's player, so you need to start concentrating on your game again. There can be no distractions. These are Ahmet's words.'

'So, where's Ahmet now? Why didn't he come?'

'He can't be seen with us. Too many questions would be asked. So, are you interested in meeting the driver or not?' he asks.

I stop and think for a moment. Maybe the driver knows the truth about what happened to Lewis. I have nothing to lose. I take a deep breath.

'Okay,' I say.

Hamza stands up and nods slightly.

'Come to the police station at ten tonight. My office is on the third floor. Don't tell a soul about this!' he warns.

20

'WE saw the whole thing! You can't deny it!' Rupert had said slyly, with the others frowning and nodding from behind.

It was at the sixth form Summer Ball, at the time I had been dating a girl called Anne-Marie Andrews. Unfortunately, that particular year no guests from outside the school were allowed to attend the Ball- although I hear they changed it a couple of years later- therefore, Anne-Marie couldn't attend. Consequently, I was just a single guy at a party.

I always blamed myself for what I'd done. But now looking back, giving a seventeen-year-old a couple of bottles of beer, endless glasses of punch from the fishbowl and expecting him to behave when surrounded by sixth form-girls wearing revealing dresses, was just not realistic.

Vicky Bryant was her name. She was in my art and sports classes. For two years there was endless flirting and when I say endless, I mean flirting that hadn't led anywhere until the Summer Ball. In the crowded hall we eventually bumped into each other. Just as well, as there was no one else to talk to. Almost everyone was paired off, either dancing… or kissing. Mr. Weber, the deputy head, was marching around like a patrol officer, pulling apart the romantics who got too close and giving them verbal warnings.

'This has got to be the worst DJ I've ever heard,' said Vicky, holding a glass of the cheap wine.

'Is the school actually paying for this? Because I'd want my money back!' I added.

'Well, we might as well enjoy it,' she replied as she placed her arms around my neck.

We were at the very corner of the hall, getting lost in a slow dance, and a passionate kiss followed. Everyone was lost in their own moment, so I didn't think anyone had seen us, although I felt incredibly guilty afterward. I dared not mention anything to Anne-Marie, not knowing Rupert Andrews, an old friend of hers (and one of her many admirers) had witnessed us kissing.

'I'm not denying it,' I kept telling him. 'It was just a stupid mistake.'

'Damn right it was stupid. Are you going to tell her? Or shall I have the pleasure?' Rupert had threatened.

I punched him hard, knocking him to the ground. He ended up with a broken nose and I ended up with no girlfriend. Manning up, I did confess to Anne-Marie what I had done. That was the last ever conversation I had with her. History certainly has a funny way of repeating itself. I worry if I tell Aysha about my ex-fiancé turning up on my doorstep and kissing me, she would never forgive me, even if it was against my will. I contemplate whether she would be out of my life if I did tell her, just like Anne-Marie.

*   *   *

I park in the police station carpark and make my way inside. It's five to ten and the place is quiet. An officer sits at the front desk and asks if I need help. I thank him as I walk past, continuing around the corner and up the stairs. On reaching the third floor I make my way along the corridor, past a dozen empty rooms, most with the doors wide open.

Eventually, I locate Hamza in a room on the left, sipping Turkish coffee and staring at his phone's screen. When he notices me, he invites me in and asks if I would like a coffee. I thank him and pass. He tells me to wait for a couple of minutes so he can finish his.

After a twenty-minute wait, ten that involved Hamza finishing his coffee and another ten talking on his phone, I follow him down to the cells. The dampness and the mould odours hit me hard down here, reminding me of when I was locked up for the night. A bored-looking police officer sits at a desk, yawning while fidgeting on his phone. He looks up and briefly acknowledges us. Hamza grabs the chain of keys from in front of him.

We continue along the corridor where the cells are. In the first one on the right, at the far corner, sits a man on the floor, leaning his back up against the wall. I examine him carefully, trying to see if I recognize him from the night I'd been forced into the car, but to be honest, if I'd passed him on the street, I wouldn't have a clue who he was.

After about four attempts, Hamza eventually finds the correct key and unlocks the cell door with the large set of jingling keys. As we walk in, I notice a large guard materialises outside the cell, who is easily taller than six feet and is just as wide.

'Ok, Manov, speak!' Hamza orders the man harshly.

'You got a packet of Parliaments?' he asks with a strong Eastern European accent, as he forces himself up from the ground.

'Guard!' calls Hamza aggressively. 'Move Manov back into cell eight!'

'N-N-NO!' stutters Manov in horror, suddenly looking off-colour, putting his hands up mercifully, as if a gun is being aimed at him. 'I can do without the cigarettes for now.'

'So, are you ready to talk?'

'Sure.'

'Well, in that case, cancel cell eight,' sniffs Hamza, shooting him a frowning stare.

I'm really curious to know what's in cell eight, but dare not ask. Whatever it is, it evidently put a lot of fear into Manov, who is trembling uncontrollably.

'He's all yours,' Hamza says to me, taking a step back.

'This better be quick! I feel uncomfortable with this meeting!' splutters Manov.

'I don't give a shit about your comfort. My career is on the line!' I say to him with frustration.

'Then speak! What do you wanna know?' he spits, trying to make himself comfortable on the concrete bed.

'Where's Lewis?' I ask.

He keeps silent; The question makes him uncomfortable. He starts to fidget, picking at the wall with his little finger.

'We're waiting for an answer!' says Hamza scornfully from behind me.

Tears start pouring down from Manov's eyes.

'Please… don't make me do this… they'll kill me too when I get out… I know they will!' he sniffs, wiping his cheeks with the back of his hands.

'Your secret is safe here. Whatever you say about Mr. V, no one will ever find out,' I assure him, trying to stay calm, although I'm feeling impatient about what he has to say.

For the first time, he acknowledges me as we lock eyes. I nod and try to raise a smile. It seems to pay off, as he starts to talk.

'He told us that we must make sure Lewis is inside. Thousand euros each was on offer. But I didn't care about the money. I was more concerned about my family. He threatened to hurt them if we didn't go through with it. I have a two-year-old daughter.'

Manov starts to become fidgety, as he nervously confesses to how the gang had burnt down the apartment of Lewis's penthouse in Majorca. He explains lit bottles of petrol were thrown at the windows during the night.

'We'd prepared so many the fire had started almost instantly. Some bottles smashed against the walls. Others hit the windows, causing the whole building to go up like a

177

bonfire,' he explains as he uncomfortably drips with sweat, red-faced.

'Was Lewis, definitely in?' I ask.

He nods.

'Jesus,' I say, feeling nauseous.

'You burnt an entire apartment block, and there were no bodies recovered. Not even Lewis'. How do you explain that?' asks Hamza.

'It was a newly constructed building. Most the flats were empty,' explains Manov.

'And Lewis?' I ask.

Manov shrugs.

'Well, I guess that's that,' says Hamza.

'Just one more thing that doesn't make sense,' I say.

Manov looks at me blankly.

'Why go through all this trouble?'

'What do you mean?'

'Mr. V is doing everything he can to become my representative and trying so hard to get me into a Premier League club. I am just a standard Championship player with no Premier League experience. So why me? He even got you to come all the way here, just because he won a bet to become my agent? Something just doesn't add up.'

Manov raises a smile.

'Gambling with Lewis was just a small part of a bigger plan.'

'*A bigger plan*?'

'It's all part of a game... or more like a bet.'

'What do you mean?'

'It's quite simple. There are quite a few contestants… or let's call them businesspeople. They all bet a million pounds. Whoever succeeds in getting a lower-league player into a Premier League club, wins the big prize. We are talking millions!'

'That sounds ridiculous,' says Hamza.

'Does it? Even with millions of pounds up for grabs?' replies Manov. 'I don't think so.'

'So that explains why he is trying so hard,' I say.

'All I can say is good luck. He won't stop until he gets what he wants, which are your agency rights, then he won't stop until he gets you into a Premier League club.'

'And if he fails?' I ask.

'He never fails,' replies Manov.

As we are walk back up the stairs, I notice a silver device, hidden in Hamza's fist.

He notices me catching a glimpse of it.

'This is solid evidence,' he says, looking proud. 'I will send the recording of the conversation to the UK. police!'

21

April 3rd

THE sun shines from the east, revealing the green in her eyes, and turning her dark hair hazel. Strolling down from my rented apartment, we pass the stadium and head down towards town. During the weekdays, this part of Kyrenia is calm, only getting busy at the weekends, and that's only because of the matches.

Uncertain whether it's a good idea, I decide to tell Aysha about the prison visit, making her promise not to tell anyone.

'If I were you, I wouldn't go back to the UK. in a hurry. At least you're safe here,' she reassures me, taking out a sunglasses case from her bag, clicking the box open and putting on a pair of dark shades. 'Dad's got your back. He trusts you.'

'That's good to know. He's a good man,' I say.

She nods.

'So… what's the plan for today?' I ask.

'Well, as it's my day off, I don't want to spend it walking aimlessly around Kyrenia,' she replies, with a grin.

'Then what do you have in mind?'

She turns and glances at me, with her large shades covering most of her face, resembling the eyes of a giant fly.

'Have you ever been strawberry picking?' she asks.

'No. You feel like eating strawberries?'

'Sure! Let's pick some. And I can show you Mavi Köşk[15] too!'

'What's that?'

'You'll see! But you'll need your passport. As it's on military property, you can't enter without it.'

'I have training at six,' I remind her, looking at my watch, which reads ten-thirty.

'If we leave now, we should be okay! Quick! Get your passport!'

'You're crazy,' I laugh.

On the way, Aysha explains that Güzelyurt is a town located in the northwest of Cyprus. It is the capital of the Güzelyurt district, an agricultural area and a market town, famous for its citrus fruits, which consists mainly of oranges, lemons, and grapefruit. Back in the Middle Ages, however, the city was called Morphou, and even back then, the area grew more than half of the island's citrus fruits.

---

[15] Mavi Köşk: The Blue Mansion, is a museum, built by Paulo Paolides, lawyer to Archbishop Makarios III.

Further west in the Tilliria region, along the shores of Morphou Bay, there is a small village known as Yeşilirmak-where in the springtime both tourists and locals flock from all over to visit the strawberry fields, handpicking their fair share of strawberries- although, some prefer to buy them from the stands.

'You know the homemade lemonade that you like?' she asks, observing the greenery outside, which in a couple of months will have dried out due to the hot Mediterranean climate. 'They make that in Güzelyurt with local lemons.'

The weather in Cyprus this time of year is a mixture of sun and rain. And the drive to Yeşilırmak has been a reminder of that. It lightly starts to drizzle.

'It'll pass. The sky is clear ahead,' she says, eyeing the horizon as we pass the turnoff to Güzelyurt and continue towards Yeşilırmak.

'Aysha?' I say, in a moment of braveness, wanting to tell her about Jessie.

'Yes?' she replies.

"Tell her, Andrew! Andrew! Don't be such a coward and tell her what happened!" a voice in my head keeps prompting me.

'Nothing… I forgot what I was going to say. Beautiful scenery.'

"Coward!"

'Isn't it just? Couldn't have been *that* important then.'

'What's that?'

'What you were going to say. If you've forgotten, it couldn't have been that important,' she says.

I don't answer. She is right about one thing. It isn't important, but I know she wouldn't see it that way. It was an attempt to sabotage my relationship with her and also destroy my career at Doğan. Although I know she needs to know about Jessie's visit, I just can't bring myself to tell her.

It takes forty-five minutes to reach Yeşilırmak. Instantly, we come across a strawberry farm. Surprisingly, six cars and a coach are parked along the road at this time of the morning, which I didn't expect to see on a weekday. This is an indication of the number of people visiting, especially at weekends, bearing in mind there are many of these farms.

I park Aysha's Range Rover at an empty spot near to the farm's entrance. A man with an old grey cap and a red t-shirt greets us. Next to him on a wooden table that needs varnishing rest hundreds of plastic containers.

'Hello! Welcome!' he smiles.

'Two please,' says Aysha.

'That's forty Lira,' he says, handing over two containers.

I get out two twenties and hand them to him.

'Thank you. Please enjoy!' he grins.

'Well, I guess we'd better get picking,' Aysha suggests, handing me one of the containers.

She leads the way into the field that is covered with thousands of bright green strawberry plants disappearing into the horizon, filling the air with their sweet smell.

I watch as she leans down next to one of them, pushing its leaves out of the way, where beneath six strawberries hide, two of which are green, one a whitish-pink, and the other three a

183

bright red. Delicately she picks the three red ones. Instead of throwing one in the container, she bites into it.

'Tastes amazing!' she exclaims, closing her eyes with satisfaction.

'Don't they need to be washed first?' I ask.

She smiles.

'You haven't lived!' she says, as she moves onto the next plant. The more I get to know her, the more I see her competitive side. I'm sure she's the same at work too, always giving a hundred percent in everything she does.

Being experienced, she fills her container a lot quicker than I do. Soon we're halfway down the field with containers full of bright red strawberries.

We head back to the car, treating ourselves to a couple more strawberries, then place the two containers on the back seat.

'Very courageous of you to eat without washing,' she teases.

'You're a bad influence.'

We end up hugging. Her lips taste of strawberry.

A strange feeling lingers as if we're being watched, but I put it down to paranoia. All these recent events put me on edge. I try not to ruin the moment. This is just what we both needed, especially Aysha, as she seems happy with the change of scenery.

'Where to next?' I say, holding her tight in my arms.

'Mavi Koşk,' she says softly, feeling the warmth of her body pressing against mine.

'Mavi-?'

Suddenly I catch sight of a man on a motorbike taking multiple pictures of us. Fully kitted with biking gear, his black helmet covers his face. Ignoring the fact that we are looking right at him, he doesn't move and continues to press the button, with every *click*, filling up his phone with our photos.

'What do you want?' I cry, walking up to him.

Hurriedly he places the phone into his arm's pocket, zips it shut, and whizzes away before I get any nearer.

'Probably paparazzi,' says Aysha, looking concerned.

'That *would* be the best-case scenario,' I say, hurriedly heading back to the car. 'On the other hand, he could be working for Mr. V!'

I jump inside and start the engine.

'I hope you're not thinking of chasing him!' she says, sitting down on the passenger seat.

I don't say anything for a moment. This was no paparazzi, nor was it a photographer working for a local newspaper. I've been here long enough to know the difference by now. If a photographer wants to take pictures, they usually ask and assist with the poses they are looking for, wanting the best possible outcome to show their boss. Without a doubt, this was someone working privately, someone who was watching our every move.

'No, I'm not thinking of chasing him. Realistically speaking, I'd never catch him up.'

As tempting as it sounds, I can't deny I don't think about it. But her off-road tank would never match the nippy motorbike on these narrow roads.

'I memorised the number plate if that helps,' says Aysha, with a wink.

'You're a genius!'

Pressing the start button, I turn on the car engine and drive east, the same direction that the motorbike headed.

'Need to act fast, though. We need to notify someone quick, as it is a rented motorbike,' she adds.

The only person I can think of calling is Mustafa Hamza. After a couple of rings, he answers. I tell him about what happened and then give him the number-plate. All he can do is check the renter's information with the rental company.

'I will let you know,' he says.

'Thank you! '

'But don't get too excited. They could have given a fake I.D. Are you sure it wasn't just a fan?'

'This was no fan. As long as they're not working for Mr. V, I don't care who they are.'

'And if they are, then what can we do?' he asks.

I take a deep breath. 'I really don't know. Might be worth talking to them.'

Hamza is silent for a moment, then says, 'We can't force someone to talk against their will. He only took some pictures. It's barely an offence.'

'Sure,' I say, disappointingly.

'I'll call you if I find anything,' he says.

I thank him and hang up.

'We shouldn't let this ruin our day. There are still some interesting places to visit around here,' says Aysha, trying to lighten the air and get me back to the good spirits I was in earlier. But I know I won't be unless I'm satisfied the photographer wasn't working for Mr. V.

✵ ✵ ✵

Turning left, we pass the city centre and go over a small bridge, arriving in an open area. Altogether, I count five restaurants. A beach is visible down the road. Parking the car nearby, we walk towards the furthest restaurant, which is festooned with grapevines.

'The beach is called Asmah Plaj for obvious reasons. When translated into English, it means Vine Beach,' Aysha explains, moving her wind-blown hair to one side away from her face.

'That's a lot of vines,' I say, surprised by the sheer quantity.

'It certainly is! In fact, according to the Guinness Book of Records, it is the largest grapevine in the whole of Cyprus.'

A couple of tourists sitting under the vine enjoy draught beer, while others opt for the local lemonade. I am fully aware I shouldn't be drinking before training. However, I don't need much persuasion from Aysha to join her for a pint, accompanied by a hellim and tomato toastie. The alcohol helps to calm my nerves, but I still feel some level of paranoia. Aysha certainly notices me looking around at the other customers with suspicion.

'I thought you'd be more used to having your photo taken by now,' she says, taking a bite of the toasted sandwich.

I don't answer and sip some beer.

'Unless you had a bad experience in the past or something,' she adds.

I almost choke on the beer.

'Who said anything about a bad experience?' I ask, feeling irritated by her comments.

The image of the cyclist comes flashing back. Then there was the driver who photographed Jessie kissing me- although that one I hadn't noticed at the time- I start feeling fatigued.

'I just think you're overreacting. Try to calm down,' says Aysha, surprised by my reaction.

'The mob forced me into a car… the media are blaming me for Lewis' disappearance… my mum and aunt were tied up and could have been killed! And now I'm being followed! How can I calm down, Aysha?'

She takes a deep breath and composes herself.

'You're right, but you are only upsetting yourself right now. Everything will sort itself out. It always does in the end,' she says, serenely.

She's right, I think to myself. *She's absolutely amazing. What am I doing raising my voice at her?*

'Sorry, I didn't mean to snap at you. There's been so much weight on my shoulders lately,' I say apologetically.

'I know,' she says, holding on to my arm. 'It will all blow over.'

We don't say much after that and finish our toasted-sandwiches and beers.

* * *

After having lunch under the island's largest grapevine, Aysha navigates, showing the way to St. Mamas' Monastery in Güzelyurt. The place is relatively secluded, making parking easy. A light breeze blows, carrying the fresh smell of lemon and oranges all mixed as one, making me realize why Güzelyurt is considered the citrus capital of the island.

'I thought this might be a good place to stop on the way to Mavi Köşk. They sell bottles of the local lemonade outside the monastery,' she says.

An older man materialises near one of the lemonades stands, waving his free hand, while the other is holding what appears to be an unusual homemade walking stick.

'Osman Dayı[16]!' says Aysha with excitement. 'He's my mum's first cousin. Come! I'll introduce you.'

Running up to him, she gives him a hug and a kiss and mumbles something in Turkish. She then turns and waves me over. The man winces as he focuses his poor vision towards me. He then smiles and puts out his hand to shake mine.

'So, you're the famous footballer the whole family is fussing over,' he says light-heartedly, in well-spoken English.

'I don't know why that is,' I say, as he gives my hand a hard grip and over-shakes it until it starts to ache.

---

[16] Dayı: Uncle (in the Turkish language)

'As long as our girl is happy and the team is winning, no one will get the cane,' he says, playfully swinging the oddly shaped walking stick, making both Aysha and I laugh.

'You always have to stay positive in life!' he continues. 'That was drummed into us at school. I went to a private English college in Nicosia, back in the early sixties. There were students of all nationalities. English, Turkish, Greek… even a couple of French and German. I was one of the naughty ones… received the end of the cane on quite a few occasions.'

'Luckily, *that* practice was long terminated when I was at school,' I say.

'Luckily. So… you've come here to take a look at our local treasure, huh?' Osman says, looking over at St. Mamas'.

'Aysha is giving me a tour of the area. We've already been strawberry picking.'

'Perfect time for it!'

'We got ourselves a couple of bucketsful,' Aysha adds. 'And now we've come to look at St. Mamas.'

'St. Mamas might not be huge, but it has a long history. It's miraculous how these ancient buildings hold up forever and are stronger than the modern ones today. They were much better architects for sure. No offence,' he says to Aysha, who smiles back and says, 'None taken.'

We follow him as he limps towards the monastery, with what's left of the white hair on his balding head dancing in the spring breeze.

'The side portals and the columns are the most ancient part of the building from an earlier gothic church that was built by the Lusignans. The church that is inside the monastery itself is originally a Byzantine building. It's been reconstructed many times over the centuries. Most of the buildings date back to the eighteenth century. That is also when the large dome on the top was added,' explains Osman, pointing his walking stick at the dome on top.

We enter the building through the north door. On the left rests the tomb of St. Mamas, surrounded with votive offerings. From the room, I get a chill causing a slight shiver passing through my body and feel unusual energy that feels calm and vigorous at the same time.

'Holes were bored in the sides of the tomb during the Ottoman rule. It was believed that treasure was hidden inside. But instead, a type of oil leaked out at irregular intervals. Word has it that this nectar calmed stormy seas,' explains Osman with a chuckle as he shakes his head at the thought of it.

'I'm not one for old wives' tales,' he adds almost apologetically, as we examine some of the colourful treasures resting around the tomb.

After a look around the monastery, we head out.

'How's the family doing?' he asks Aysha when we are outside.

'Same old. Dad is busy with the club. And mum, she's either at home trying out new recipes in the kitchen or busy being a socialite.'

'Nothing ever changes,' grins Osman.

He then stops and turns, shoots me a look, and then glances at Aysha. 'Walk me to my car,' he says.

Aysha and I both look at each other blankly and shrug.

'Sure.'

His classic red Mercedes is not too far from where we'd parked and is in mint condition as if it hasn't left the dealership yet. He digs his hand into his pocket, takes out a bunch of keys and slots one into the keyhole in the boot and clicks it open. Aysha looks just as surprised as I do when she sees what's inside. Enough bottles of the local lemonade are inside to fill up an entire fridge. Osman reaches in and grabs two bottles of the glistening bright yellow squash and hands them over.

'Thank you,' I say, assuming one is for Aysha, but it turns out I'm mistaken.

He also passes two bottles to her.

'And here are yours,' he says with a smile.

She thanks him.

'That's extremely generous of you,' I say.

'Don't mention it. You two take care now and have a safe trip back to Kyrenia,' he waves, as we walk back to the car.

I feel a lot happier compared to when we had first arrived. So much so I don't care about the photographer on the motorbike anymore. Aysha also looks happier.

'Osman Dayı is a character, isn't he?' she remarks.

'You can say that again,' I say, and we both laugh.

Mavi Koşk (the Blue Mansion) rests in a secluded area a couple of kilometres away from the main road on the outskirts of Çamlıbel and is probably one of the most eccentric sights

192

found in Cyprus. It's so well hidden that it's not visible on approach- but somehow has a spectacular view of the surrounding landscapes from its top floor balcony.

We enter the premises and park close to the mansion, leaving our passports with a soldier on duty at the car park entrance.

When inside, a couple of guards hand over information sheets in English for the tour. Mostly, the information describes the features inside the rooms as well as giving a brief insight into the history of the place.

One feature I find fascinating is the soundproof leather curtains dividing the living room from the study. Even today, that would be somewhat of a luxury.

Rather than looking around a museum, it feels like walking around someone's home in the sixties. It suddenly occurs to me why it's called the Blue Mansion. The window frames, carpets, and curtains, as well as the furniture all, have a definite light blue theme.

According to the information, it is believed that a Greek Cypriot named Paulo Paolides had built the mansion in 1957. Paolides was rumoured to work for the Italian mafia, smuggling guns into the country. However, it is said that he escaped through a secret tunnel hidden inside during the 1974 conflict.

Unfortunately, taking photos in the house is prohibited, but free on the balcony at the roof. And what a view for it! The surrounding landscape is just phenomenal. I've never seen anything as picturesque. Now it makes sense why Paulo had picked this spot to build his fortress. As well as the privacy and the beautiful surroundings, it's a perfect place for a lookout.

'Our first selfie,' says Aysha, raising her mobile.

'Why not,' I answer, snuggling up close to her and smiling at the camera.

She takes a couple of snaps.

I take out my phone and see two missed calls from Hamza. I call him back.

'Andrew! I've got a name!' he says with excitement.

'Who is it?'

'Boyan Bakalov. He presented a Bulgarian I.D. for the bike. Flew into Ercan from London a couple of days ago.'

'Did you find out where he's staying?' I ask anxiously.

'The hotel address he gave is fake. The motorbike was found abandoned near the border, which he crossed an hour ago. So, he is out of our reach, and I don't think he'll be crossing back to the north anytime soon. But they will keep me posted if he does.'

I thank Hamza and hang up. Aysha worriedly stares at me, and I sense myself worriedly glancing back at her. Things get worse when I notice a picture message from Noeweir Tuhide. Hesitantly, I bring the picture up.

Aysha and I are eating strawberries outside the farm. A message beneath reads, *"How are you enjoying Mavi Koşk?"*

'What is it?' asks Aysha, anxiously.

Ignoring her, I look around, my heart beats faster by the second. There are about ten people up here- maybe slightly more- they are all tourists. Some are taking pictures, as others are lost in their information sheets, reading about Paulo's

194

unconventional life. None of them look suspect, but someone here- one of these people- must be sending information to Mr. V.

A man wearing glasses and a cream-coloured cap, stares out into the view, clinching his phone tightly in his left hand- he looks out of place- can it be *him*?

'You're making *me* nervous,' says Aysha, also looking around suspiciously.

'Wait here,' I tell her and walk towards the edge of the balcony.

I stand next to the man. He doesn't notice me.

'Nice view,' I say, looking out at the mystifying landscape.

'Ja, very guut. Wunderbar!' he exclaims nodding.

'Where are you from?' I ask friendlily.

'From the Netherlands,' he says with a smile.

A lady comes over and grabs him by the arm.

'Oke, schat?' she says.

'Ja,' he answers.

'Have a guud day,' he says as they walk away.

'Likewise,' I reply.

'You're being paranoid,' Aysha says from behind.

'Let's go,' I tell her.

'Good idea,' she breathes, looking uncomfortable.

We head back to Kyrenia. Neither of us hardly says a word on the way back.

22

April 4th

EXHAUSTED from yesterday's road trip, followed by what I can only describe as an extra tiring training session, it's no surprise getting up this morning has been somewhat of a challenge, especially, being woken up by an incoming call. Nonchalantly, I reach out and grab my phone- forcing my eyes open, I focus on the screen. It's a withheld number. I wait, not wanting to answer it- I can't deal with Mr. V at this time of the morning- then again, it could also be Alp. So, I take the chance and feel relieved to hear his voice on the other end, even if he does sound off and not his usual self.

'Meet me at the George at half ten,' he grunts.

'Is everything all right?'

He's already hung up.

The time is nine forty-five, which gives me a good three-quarters of an hour to get ready and be there. I keep asking myself why he wants to meet at The George on a weekday and not his office. Fearing the worst, I sense something isn't right- I can guess what it is- the time has come for confrontation.

Spectacular traffic slows life down in Kyrenia. I join the long train of slow-moving vehicles heading towards the city centre. By half ten, I'm parked at the Baldöken car park opposite The George.

The café is relatively empty at this time of the morning, and there is only one customer- Hasan Alp. As always, a handful of waiters hover around. They greet me with welcoming smiles as I walk in. Alp, however, isn't as welcoming. He sits with his dark sunglasses, looking rough and glum, and his expression doesn't change when I approach his table.

'Hello, Mr. Alp,' I say.

Jerking his head forward, he indicates for me to sit.

I sit myself down opposite him.

He sniffs, gathering a bunch of newspapers scattered around the table and chucks them in front of me.

'This has now become a personal matter,' he grunts.

I notice in the English tabloids, large colourful pictures of Jessie giving me a hug and a kiss. A kiss that can be mistaken for a passionate moment between two lovers.

One of the paper's headline reads *"Pablo Rossi's Ex-Girlfriend, Jessie Fell, Goes Back to Ex-Fiancé Footballer."*

The other is vaguer and simply states, *"Romance in Cyprus."*

"Love Rat Footballer Plays Home and Away," reads another paper with another picture of Aysha and me hugging after the strawberry picking. I'm amazed at how much effort went into these.

'This is not how it seems-'

'Keep away from my daughter,' Alp hisses with anger.

I take a deep sigh, uncertain how I can get out of this mess.

'It was a setup. She turned up at my doorstep!'

'Aysha is extremely upset. Don't you dare go near her again!'

A waiter comes up to our table to ask us if we'd like anything. Alp waves him away: *Don't disturb us!*

As the waiter walks away, I feel Alp shooting me a stare behind his dark shades.

'She will get married to her fiancé' as planned! Not that it's any of your business, Ashford. So, stay away from her!'

His words, like daggers, dig deep into my heart, as I start to feel breathless.

'Umut?' I grumble in disbelief. 'The guy's an idiot! Her life will be ruined if you force her to get back together with him!'

'That's rich coming from *you*!' he slams. 'At least he comes from a good respectable family, and I can be sure she won't get hurt anymore!'

He points at the scattered papers in front of me, thinks for a moment, then adds, 'And who said anything about forcing?'

'No!' I say, shaking my head in disbelief.

I get my phone out. 'I will call her right now and explain everything to her! And I know she'll understand!'

Alp doesn't clinch, 'Which part of *stay away from my daughter* didn't you understand?' he asks.

'She deserves to know the truth!'

He removes his sunglasses, places them on the table, and gives me a look as if to say, *"I dare you to."*

After waiting for a long shaky minute, the call goes onto voicemail. Alp leans towards me slightly and snarls, 'Stay away.'

Defeated, I take a closer look at the papers, turning over some of their pages. Two cleverly displayed pictures side by side shows Jessie's arms wrapped around me, forcing the kiss. On the other, Aysha and I are hugging and kissing outside the strawberry farm.

However, the second paper vexes me the most. A picture taken at Jashan's by the couple who were supposed Luton fans. The small print reads, *"Ashford now lives a luxurious life in Northern Cyprus and is wanted for questioning by the UK. police for the disappearance of his agent, Lewis Orland."*

'I will be *brutally* honest with you,' adds Alp, puffing on a large Cohiba cigar. 'I have my suspicions regarding Lewis. And I strongly believe you're hiding something.'

I stare at him for a long moment, trying to get my head around what he just said. I do my best to stay calm.

'Listen, I know you're mad because you think I cheated on your daughter. And as bad as it may seem, I swear I didn't do anything to hurt her! But what you just said about Lewis is a very serious accusation. One I hope you don't truly believe!'

'Is that so?' he grunts dismissively.

Standing up, he abandons his half-burnt cigar in the large cigar-ashtray.

'Only a couple of games left until you're a free agent,' he says.

'I've been set-up! You have to believe me!' I beg. 'I would never do anything to hurt Aysha.'

He ignores me, throws a twenty Lira note on the table, and walks away.

❋ ❋ ❋

A distant memory comes rushing back from when I was only fifteen. I sat on a desk in the empty classroom, holding back tears, as Mrs. Ashworth, who taught me maths, sat opposite, facing me.

'You and your big mouth, Andrew,' she gently scolded me. 'But in no way does it deserve a month's worth of detention. Just what is Mr. Wells playing at?'

Earlier that day, Mr. Wells, the art teacher, who couldn't draw (or paint) if his life depended on it, proudly showed the class his latest oil painting of a duck in a lake he'd just finished painting.

'So, what do you think?' he asked the class, delicately laying the canvas on a chair, while all the students blankly looked on in silence. Well, all but one. I just couldn't resist it.

'It's no Van Gogh, sir,' I blurted out, not thinking of the consequences, as you hardly do at that age. The entire classroom filled with loud laughter. The only person who wasn't amused was Mr. Wells. He never did have a sense of humour. Nor was he fond of me. His large magnified eyes, surrounded by thick grey-framed glasses, just stared at me blankly.

'Very amusing, Mr. Ashford,' he said coldly. 'Let's see how amusing a month's worth of detention will be!'

My world had fallen apart until I went to talk to my mentor, Mrs. Ashworth. Speaking to my football coach wouldn't do much good, as the academy wasn't linked with the school.

'I'll miss football training and three games!' I cried to Mrs. Ashworth, who looked on with some sympathy, knowing how important football was to me.

'I'll talk to him,' she suggested.

She managed to get the detentions reduced to only five days.

However, I still found myself in the headmaster's office for a good old grilling that involved a lecture on discipline- which I was reminded of during the meeting with Alp. Even though the reasons were poles apart, it was the coldness that made the two confrontations bear a similarity. And yet they both had a clear message.

"Stay out of trouble…

Stay away from my daughter!"

Darker clouds replace the grey ones- it starts to drizzle- with the rain getting heavier by the second. I watch Alp walk away and slowly follow him towards the car park. I try calling Aysha again, but she doesn't accept my call, putting it on to engaged.

'For Christ's sake!' I gasp to myself, walking faster.

A loud buzz of a motorcycle exhaust rattles the square, causing a flock of pigeons that were feeding on the ground, to scatter in all directions in a sheer moment of panic. Barking aggressively, a dog, to which Kyrenia town centre is home to so many, jumps towards the motorbike, agitated by its noise. Although it all happens in a flash, my mind plays the moment in slow motion.

To avoid colliding with the large mongrel, the bike swerves to the side, not taking into account the freshly wet road. The chunky BMW motorcycle skids towards Alp, hitting him hard and flings him onto an oncoming red car, which has luckily managed to stop- or even if it hasn't, is driving incredibly slowly. The motorbike slides on its side, rotating like one of those fidget-toys. The cyclist slowly gets up and appears to be unhurt but in shock.

Alp lies in a pool of increasing blood, unconscious and uncontrollably shivering. His leg is rotated- facing the direction it shouldn't, with one of his shoulders a lot lower than the other- his arm dislocated.

I sprint towards him.

'SOMEONE CALL AN AMBULANCE!' I scream, realizing that I don't even have the number for the emergency services in this foreign country that has become my home. 'PLEASE! SOMEONE CALL-'

'Okay! Ambulance on way!' cries a man with struggling English. He is the driver of the red car. He looks pale.

Alp starts to shudder more intensely, losing more blood. I can't even imagine the pain he's going through; it must be something beyond pain where the state of shock kicks in.

Covered with both rainwater and blood, he is looking paler and is getting incredibly colder.

I remove my jacket to cover him, not sure how much difference it will make, but he needs to stay as warm as possible until the ambulance gets here.

'Relax Hasan! Help's on its way!' I assure him as I place my jacket over his body, unsure if he can hear me.

The crowd increases with many passers-by stopping out of curiosity. A couple of police officers were on duty nearby and come to question the motorist and the biker. They also talk to some witnesses, but for some reason, they bypass me. Luckily it doesn't take long for the ambulance to arrive.

The two paramedics- a man with large bags under his eyes and an attractive young lady, looking more eager- with the drivers' help, slide Alp onto a stretcher and wheel him into the back of the ambulance.

The male paramedic had spotted me taking my jacket back and asks if I'm the patient's friend or relative. I tell him that he's my boss: a good enough answer to get me a free pass to ride in the ambulance.

Sitting in the front passenger seat, I try calling Aysha again, this time for a completely different reason, a reason she might regret not answering.

I watch the power of the sirens work their magic, as the other vehicles make way and the flashing of speed cameras mean nothing. We head out of Kyrenia.

'Which hospital are we going to?' I ask the driver.

'Nalbantoğlu in Lefkoşa,' he mumbles, not taking his eyes off the road ahead.

'How's he doing back there?' I ask, concerned about how Alp's holding up.

The driver slightly shrugs and doesn't answer, so I patiently wait as worry eats me alive for the rest of the journey.

After about ten minutes, we arrive at Burhan Nalbantoğlu, the only government hospital in the north of Nicosia. Without further ado, Hasan is rushed into the dimness of a building that hasn't seemed to change much since the beginning of its days and would most certainly give any NHS hospital a sense of luxury.

I get asked to wait at a waiting area outside the Accident and Emergency Unit, filled with anxious faces. After a twenty minutes wait, my name gets called. A policeman with a pen and pad walks up to me.

'Andrew Ashford?'

'Yes.'

'My name is Özgür Yılmaz. I'm with the traffic department. I'd like to ask you some questions regarding the accident,' he says.

'Sure,' I answer, feeling grim as the moment plays back in my mind.

I tell him exactly what I saw.

'So, would you say the bike was speeding?' he asks.

'I wouldn't call it speeding. Its exhaust was very loud. So loud that it irritated the dog.'

'I see,' he says, jotting down my every word on the pad. 'And the car?'

'What about it?'

'Was it speeding?'

I take a deep breath, trying to blank out the disfigured image of Alp lying on the ground in the pool of blood.

'It wasn't,' I answer.

He thanks me. As he's leaving, I stop him and ask how Alp is. He says a doctor should be with me shortly, but the last he heard an emergency operation was being performed.

After an anxious half an hour wait, the door from the Emergency Unit flings open and a man in a white coat appears. He calls out my name. I hurry towards him. He says his name is Dr. Ali Ozan- a neurosurgeon.

'We had to perform emergency surgery to stop the internal bleeding. He's received a severe injury to the head. It can also be seen from the radiographs and the CT scan that there are multiple fractures. He will also need some orthopaedic surgeries,' he explains.

'How's his condition?'

Dr. Ozan looks deep into my eyes; his expression sad.

'Critical,' he says.

'Can I see him?'

'I'm afraid not. He's in the Intensive Care Unit. His condition will worsen unless Rh-negative blood is found.'

'Were you there?' a voice cuts in from behind.

I turn and see Aysha standing next to her mother, Sibel. They are both pale-faced and teary-eyed.

'Yes, I was,' I say softly.

'How did it happen?' she says with a broken voice.

I shake my head. I cannot bring myself to tell her.

'Listen, follow me. You can see him through the glass,' says Dr. Ozan. 'But in the meantime, a donor with Rh-negative blood needs to be found, fast.'

As we make our way upstairs, Sibel gets out her mobile phone and starts calling her contacts. None of them seem to have the right blood type.

'I'll do it. Mine's Rh-negative,' I say.

They look at me with astonishment in their eyes.

'Great!' says Dr. Ozan. 'Quick! Fill in a form!'

Aysha and Sibel wait in a room close by ICU, while I follow Dr. Ozan to the Pathology Lab, where an obese nurse is waiting to take my blood.

Dr. Ozan leaves me in her hands. He tells me to head straight back up to ICU with the blood as soon as possible. The nurse speaks no English, and therefore, has to demonstrate for me to make a fist. At the same time, she tightens a worn looking tourniquet around my elbow, before inserting the butterfly-needle into the vein.

As I watch the bag fill up, the sight of the blood starts haunting me again, bringing back the shuddering image of Alp. I get nauseous. Taking deep breaths, I close my eyes and try to relax. I go into a state of anxiousness, but at the same time relieved, I'm able to help him.

206

A private number calls. As it cannot be Alp, I'm guessing it's Mr. V, no doubt calling to mess with my head again, to see if he can get me to return to the UK.

'You're quite the man of the moment, Andy,' he says. I can feel him smiling, enjoying every second.

'Get lost!' I cry, with anger washing over me.

'I've given you more fame, more media exposure and that's the thanks I get?'

'Let me make one thing clear, you bastard! *You* will never be my representative!'

Those words shock him- he falls silent for a couple of seconds- and I even debate with myself if he's still there.

'Andy, Andy, Andy... There's no reason for you to stay there anymore. Aysha has lost all her trust in you. Mr. Alp doesn't want you in the team. Luton have cancelled your contract. Your career is nothing but over! I promise you a fresh start! A new future!' he says with great enthusiasm.

'You haven't got much of a future either! The police will find you eventually. You assaulted my aunt and mother! Not to mention what you did to Lewis!'

He laughs a laugh that says he doesn't give a damn.

'If the police wanted to find me, they would've done by now. Don't you think?'

The nurse walks in.

'No phone... No phone!' she calls out in her broken English.

'Listen to me very carefully!' he continues. 'Unless you let me represent you, these unfortunate events will keep happening!'

'I know about the bet.'

'Bet?'

'Yes, the one you made with your friends. Whoever gets a Championship player into the Premier League, wins the prize.'

Now Mr. V sounds concerned.

'Well then, that changes things. I never thought it would come to this,' he says and hangs up.

I curse loudly- the nurse tells me to relax in her bad English.

I don't exactly know what Mr. V meant by saying *it changes things*, but I'm sure I have to watch my back now even more than before.

The bag eventually fills up with my blood. Once the nurse removes the line from my arm, I take the bag to the doctor's station outside the Intensive Care Unit, where Dr. Ozan awaits.

'I've just checked your results. The good news is your blood is compatible with the operation,' he tells me after twenty minutes.

'And is there bad news?' I ask.

'Your cholesterol is higher than average, so you have to keep an eye on that,' he answers.

Must be all the meals I've been having out, I think to myself. The meyhanes, the curries, along with everything else.

Dr. Ozan disappears into the Intensive Care Unit to check on Hasan Alp. After a ten-minute wait, I decide to head out for some fresh air and I come face to face with Aysha and Sibel- there's an uncomfortable silence. Admittedly, I'm the last person they want to see. She's been ignoring my calls, and I don't blame her. As far as she's concerned, I've cheated on her and as a result of it, the press has humiliated her even further.

Dr. Ozan walks out with a satisfied look.

'He's stable for the time being. He should pull through, thanks to you. Rh-negative blood is hard to come by. Things could have been a lot worse, considering the circumstances.'

'Thank you, doctor! Can we see him?' asks Sibel, wiping the tears from the edge of her eyes.

She then turns to me. 'Thank you!' she says.

'Best not to go near him for a couple of days, I'm afraid. He needs to rest,' explains Dr. Ozan.

Aysha puts her arms around me and gives me a big hug.

'Thank you,' she whispers into my ear, sobbing.

'He'll be okay,' I say, wrapping my arms around her.

'If it wasn't for you, we could have lost him,' she stutters, as tears run down her cheeks.

In the days that follow, she doesn't question anything about the pictures in the newspapers. Maybe it was my act of kindness that made her change her mind, or perhaps she chooses to ignore what I did by taking the easy way out. Still, I genuinely believe it's because she has trust in me- just as I trust her- and if she starts questioning the stories, that *trust* might get demolished.

As for her getting back with her ex-fiancé- it's not happening.

Sorry, Hasan Alp.

23

THE season draws to an end with only three games remaining. It's been three weeks since Alp's accident. He's doing well and on the mend. The day after his accident, I walked into a pre-match meeting, faced with an uncomfortable silence. All eyes were on me. Many things went through my mind as I made the long walk to the empty chair. I couldn't help but think how much the team hated me. As far as they were concerned, I'd cheated on the club president's daughter, and because of me, he had the accident. If it weren't for my actions, the accident would never have occurred.

Unexpectedly, Peter started slowly clapping- with Hakan joining him- followed by a couple of the other players and then Remzi. The entire team applauded. It turned out that giving blood to Alp made me somewhat of a hero, and all the accusations about cheating on his daughter erased. Forgotten!

How fickle life is, I kept telling myself. *Just like football.*

A three-one win over Küçük Kaymaklı that day put us in the driver's seat, as our two main opponents lost points. A few of the lads had already started going into holiday mode, so

Remzi gave them harsh reminders that the title could still easily slip through our fingers.

※ ※ ※

Eventually, the big day comes. A draw against Baf Ülkü Yurdu will be enough to make Doğan the North Cyprus Super League champions. Remzi walks into the changing room with a big grin on his face. A rare sight, indeed.

'The club president was discharged from hospital earlier and is now resting at home,' he tells us. 'Let's win this match and this season for him!'

Yesterday I was with Aysha and she didn't mention that he was going to be discharged today. I don't think even Alp knew when they were planning on letting him out.

A couple of days after his orthopaedic operation on his fractured femoral bone, I finally gathered up the courage to go and see him. Having no idea what to bring, I visited the supermarket on the way and got him a large bag of fruit.

Aysha offered to come with me, but I thought it'd be best to go alone. The thought of facing Alp alone was terrifying enough after our last encounter. But going with Aysha would have been suicidal after he'd warned me to stay away from her.

The hospital smell didn't help my nerves. The odour just seemed to increase my anxiety. I slowly knocked on the door and quietly crept in.

Alp lay sunk in the bed. The first thing that caught my eye was a large number of bandages covering most of his head. He also had a sling supporting his left arm with fresh plaster casts around both his left forearm and right lower leg. The room seemed very old- very eighties- with yellowing walls, almost making the hospital room I had stayed in during my injury, luxurious.

He turned and looked at me blankly as I slowly tiptoed in. I placed the bag on the bed-table in front of him.

'Got you some fruit.'

'Thanks,' he grunted.

'How're you feeling?'

'Like shit.'

I remember hesitating for a moment, as not in a hundred years would I imagine hearing Alp swear.

'You're looking a lot better than when I last saw you.'

'Is that so?' he said, almost raising a smile. 'I appreciate your help. Especially for the blood. But hey, at least you got to ride shotgun in the ambulance.'

I laughed.

'It's what any responsible person would do.'

'Well, not everyone is responsible, are they Andrew?'

I stopped and lingered on his comment for a while. Outside the noise of Nicosia's traffic- the beeping of horns, the revving of car engines- filled the old hospital room.

'I'm rarely wrong about a person, which is why I was so beaten up about the things I saw in the papers. One of your teammates came for a chat the other day. He said he'd witnessed the incident with your ex-fiancée. Turns out, it's not like the papers made it out to be.'

'I did try to tell you. But you didn't want to listen.'

'I know. I get protective when it involves my daughter. Anyway, I think I owe you an apology.'

Thank you, Peter!

With satisfaction, I'd listened to Alp apologising, admitting that he'd got it all wrong.

'But those papers,' he'd continued, with a sour face, clenching his fists because of the post-operation pain. 'Those papers are vicious!'

'Always have been. It's nothing new,' I said.

It was such a relief, a massive weight off my shoulders, to get back into Alp's good books. Not only because he is club president, but because he must approve of Aysha and me as a couple.

'Ashford,' he called as I was walking out. 'The team better become champions!'

I stopped and grinned at him.

'We will,' I answered.

That night I had the best sleep in a long time.

'Don't take this game lightly,' Ahmet translates Remzi's words, who is now looking more sincere.

One by one, Remzi makes eye contact with each player gathered around him, then continues. 'The opponents today have nothing to lose. So, don't forget your defensive duties. Always feed the wings! Make the ball do the work! Their second-choice keeper is playing. He's young… inexperienced. When you get a chance… shoot! It's a full stadium. The stands packed with fans, press… politicians. And they haven't come here to watch you lose. Doğan always goes out to win. Do it for them! And most important… do it for Alp!'

The boys- myself included- appear more psyched up after Remzi's talk. We run out on to the field, greeted by yellow and navy-blue flags waving vigorously to the sound of beating drums and loud chants. Remzi was not exaggerating when he said the stadium is packed.

Assisted by Remzi's coaching team, we do our final warm-ups and stretches. We then retire back to the changing rooms for another dose of team-talk, this one a lot shorter, followed by a pre-match rest. This time Remzi talks with each player individually, reminding what he expects of them.

He places his arm around my shoulder.

'Do what you always do, what you are best at. Shoot when you see the target. Don't fall back. Stay upfield and pressurise their defenders!' he buzzes with his broken English.

I just nod. Being fully concentrated, I don't answer.

When we're back on the pitch in our yellow and navy-blue striped home kits, strips of yellow and blue glitter paper rain down on us in their thousands. My heart starts to race, with adrenaline rushing through my veins. Lining up, one by one, we shake our opponents' hands, who are in all red. They look focused. This won't be easy.

Winning the coin toss, we get the advantage of kick-off. But unfortunately, the possession doesn't last long. Adil tries a through-pass, playing the ball short, which is collected by the opposition's midfield.

'USE THE WINGS!' yells Remzi from the sideline, but it's too late. Baf Ulkü Yurdu are already composing a dangerous attack. Their nippy left midfielder- with the number six shirt - runs up the field and chips the ball into the box, which skims Peter's hand.

The referee blows for a penalty and indicates a handball. Booing arises from the stands with angry screaming, in Turkish. I can only guess the things being shouted.

Süleyman, our keeper, is a gentle giant. He focuses on the ball. The penalty taker is half his height. For a moment, everything goes silent, even the traffic outside the stadium seems to have stopped. Confidently, the penalty taker runs up and strikes the ball- not too hard- placing it perfectly in the left corner. Süleyman lamely watches it go in. They run to their fans and celebrate exaggeratingly; anyone would think they'd won the league.

Adil apologetically claps his hands and cries, 'Heads up!'

For fifteen minutes, nothing happens to write home about, with both teams cancelling each other out. In the twentieth minute, I get my first real chance to get on the score sheet, but much to the relief of their nervous-looking keeper- the ball swerves right- away from the post- and out for a goal kick.

At half time we go into the changing rooms with our heads down. I sense the pressure is getting too much for the boys. Even a draw- a draw that would see us lift the trophy- starts to feel like a steep mountain to climb.

Remzi, red-faced, doesn't say too much. Ahmet translates.

'If that's your attitude, we don't deserve to be champions. Embarrassing!' he mutters dryly.

This time Remzi doesn't make eye contact with anyone, stares at the floor and adds, 'Has everything that we've trained for, gone out the window? Wake up! You are not on holiday yet!'

He then exits the changing room, leaving the players blankly staring at one another.

A long uncomfortable silence lingers.

'Come on! Let's do it for Alp!' says Adil, eventually, waving his fist in front of him.

The players' faces suddenly light up. 'For Alp!' they repeat.

Whether it was Remzi's cold approach that did the trick or Adil injecting a dose of passion into the team, we come out a different team compared to the one in the first half. For the first time since playing for the club, I feel an energy I've never felt before. We keep the majority of the possession and push forward. The opposition starts to crumble under pressure.

In the fifty-second minute, I receive a high cross from Adil and head the ball in. The crowd erupts into a loud cheer. I run up to celebrate with the fans- the team crowd around me.

'That makes up for my costly mistake in the first half!' Adil cries with joy, and I could have sworn I saw a tear running down his muddy cheek.

Not wanting to settle for a draw, Baf Ülkü Yurdu fights back and has a couple of chances to go on top again. It looks as if we start losing our momentum. Things get a bit lonely upfront, so I drop back to help with the defending.

A high ball is crossed in from the left-hand side, just outside our penalty box. Using the advantage of his height, Peter heads the ball away. Flying over one of their players, it looks like it's anybody's for the taking, until it bounces, changing direction and rolling towards me. Wasting no time, I sprint up the field. The crowd goes wild, giving me an extra boost of motivation. I notice their goalkeeper running out of his goal area and committing himself- leaving the goal open. I chip the ball high. It lingers in the air for a while before making its way into the goal. This time I jog back without celebrating but get surrounded by my teammates, who jump on me.

This is to be my last goal of the season. I'm substituted in the seventy-third minute, watching the remainder of the game from the subs bench. Both teams make several mistakes and the game still could have easily finished a draw, but in the eighty-fifth minute, Ismail heads another goal from a corner-kick to ensure a three-one victory.

Eventually, the final whistle blows. The title is ours! Fans start running on to the pitch, multiplying in numbers. After long celebrations, with chanting championship songs in Turkish, the team queues to receive their medals and the trophy.

When Adil raises the cup, the sound from the stands is overwhelming. Car horns and chants can even be heard outside the stadium. Eventually, it's my turn to raise the cup.

The fans sing my name. A couple of them, who are already on the pitch, lift me onto their shoulders. Although I'm buzzing with excitement that I kept my promise to Alp about helping the team win the title, at the same time, I feel anxious because of the uncertainty of next season. Will I still be here? Or will Mr. V have his way?

Remzi gives a short speech, to which no one pays attention. The season has been won- that's all that matters- so let the party begin!

The showers are somewhat rushed. Outside, the celebrations continue as the players make their way to the team bus. Long convoys of cars continuously beeping their horns with flags waving from their windows, surround the stadium and head towards the town centre.

Peter sits next to me on the bus.

'We've done it, bro,' he laughs.

'Yes, we certainly have!' I say. 'By the way. I want to thank you for talking to Alp.'

He turns and gives me a look.

'I only told him what I saw,' he whispers.

'I really appreciate it. I seem to be unlucky when it comes to relationships. At last, I've found someone I'm crazy about, who is beautiful and has a great personality… I don't want to mess it up.'

'Relationships need work.'

'True.'

'Somehow, you always seem to come out better than you went in,' he chuckles.

'Somehow,' I say with a smile.

With a clunk, the bus's engine starts. It struggles to move at first, but when it does, it delicately places itself into the convoy, heading away from the stadium, towards the city centre. Fans wearing the yellow and blue Doğan jersey, clap, as the bus passes. Some are waving flags, while others sing songs. One fan waves a plastic bag at us. The bus stops, and the front door swings open. He hands the bag to Ahmet. Adil takes it from him and pulls out a large bottle of champagne. Like a bus full of spoilt students, the players laugh and cheer. The champagne bottle is popped open. Half the bottle is emptied into the trophy and passed around for the team to enjoy.

I take a large gulp from the bottle, it's chilled, and although it's cheap champagne, it's still nice and refreshing.

The bus doesn't stop in the square as expected but continues out of town. After a couple of kilometres, it swerves unexpectedly into one of the side streets. This confuses the players, who a second ago were chanting football songs and enjoying the champagne. A couple of them ask Remzi where we are headed, as usually after the games, the club building- near the square- is the final destination. Remzi smiles and says there's been a slight change of plan on this occasion.

The bus climbs towards Bellapais and then turns right into one of the side roads before reaching the hillside village.

Whispers arise that we are headed for the club president's house.

Hidden inside a surrounding wall- made of red bricks, with a barricade of trees on the other side- is the Alp mansion. The bus beeps its horn and a large electronic gate, made of half wood and half metal, starts to open.

The place is massive, with an Olympic-sized swimming pool at the back.

I text Aysha, asking her where she is. A minute later she texts back saying she stopped off at a café near the stadium for coffee with a couple of friends, to avoid the traffic. I ask her to guess where I am, take a picture of the house and send it to her.

"You're kidding!" she replies, with the emoji of the monkey covering its face.

"Here to see the boss!"

"It's a nice gesture. Will make the boss happy," she writes back.

We get out of the bus. Hasan, who's in a wheelchair, is wheeled out to the lawn by Sibel. He looks a lot better and isn't as pale as before. The bandage around his head has been replaced with a thinner one. His arm is in plaster with a sling wrapped around it.

He waves with his free hand and forces out a weak 'Congratulations!' with a smile.

The team applauds, as Adil presents him the cup, which he reaches out to lightly touch. One by one, everyone queues to shake his hand. He thanks each player and coaching staff individually, handing them each a white envelope.

When it's my turn, he pulls me close and says, 'Really appreciate your help. Couldn't have done it without you. Lewis would have been proud… wherever he is.'

'Thank you. I'm sure he would have,' I answer.

After Sibel takes a couple of team photos with the president, he tells us there will be a championship Ball held soon and the details will be revealed in due course.

On the way back to the club building, I open the envelope. Inside, are a thousand euros in cash. Peter also has a peep inside his envelope and then zips it up in his bag.

'Very generous of him,' he says with a grin.

'I've booked a table for twenty-five at The Meyhane for tonight. I expect you all to be there!' announces Remzi from the front of the bus.

Five minutes later, I get a message from Aysha that reads, "Dinner tonight?"

To Remzi's disappointment, I apologise that I won't be able to make The Meyhane.

24

May 19th

IT seems like there is no place on the island that Aysha and I have left untouched. Once again, we are inseparable; especially now the season has come to an end. Today, we are paying a visit to Karmi, a village high up in the mountains, about ten kilometres east from Kyrenia.

I still find myself looking over my shoulder, and every time a 'withheld number' calls, my heart skips a beat. The fact that Mr. V hasn't been in touch for the last couple of weeks makes me feel more on edge, especially now the transfer window has opened. And on top of that, more stress mounts- as I get the feeling Aysha's family- especially Alp- is expecting an engagement announcement as soon as possible. The reason being: if you get into a serious relationship here, the question of marriage is on the tip of everyone's tongue. The older generation still views relationships without an engagement ring a sin.

If I were to pop the question, as my father is no longer with us, my mother would have the honour to ask Alp for Aysha's hand on my behalf. The differences in culture seem to be evaporating from generation to generation, but this one remains.

Today is my third visit to Karmi. There's always something about this place that makes me feel at home, and at the same time, homesick. It could be because it's Anglo-Mediterranean, with a large number of English expatriates. Either that, or it's where I used to live in my past life. Whatever the reason, it reminds me of my childhood. I was brought up in a small, secluded village in the Midlands. A couple of months back on my first visit, I sent a lot of photos to my mother, encouraging her to come and live out here. Still, the old bat is too stubborn and set in her ways to move anywhere.

The picturesque village had always appealed to foreigners. The Ministry of Interior and Housing saw this as an opportunity to lease the old rundown buildings mostly to the British and a small minority of Russian and German nationals.

My first visit here was with Aysha. Just like today, we'd come for a Sunday roast at one of the local pubs called The Castle Inn. That's when I decided that Karmi is a place I wouldn't mind living if I did settle here permanently.

'One of my friends is an estate agent. She says there's a place for sale further up the mountain,' says Aysha, sprinkling some mint sauce over her roast lamb.

'Really?'

'Yes, maybe we can have a look at it.'

'Maybe,' I say.

Dreaming about having property up here is one thing; however, putting it into action is another. It would guarantee a stronger tie with Cyprus, and this is exactly what Aysha wants.

I take my phone out of my pocket and place it on the table. There's a message from Ahmet.

"We need to meet up. It's urgent," it reads,

"Where are you?" I reply.

"With Mustafa at Cafe de Harbour."

"I'm in Karmi. What is it that's so urgent?"

"Meet us here as soon as you can. We'll wait for you," he writes back.

Aysha is not impressed with Ahmet's demanding attitude, but curious to know why they would urgently want to meet me, especially on a Sunday.

Both men have been hanging around the harbour, sitting close to the yachts, having a beer and enjoying the late spring sun. Although they try not to show it, they seem a little uncomfortable I've brought Aysha along. Ahmet forces a smile at his boss's daughter and asks if we'd like anything to eat or drink. We thank him and tell him we are stuffed from the rushed lunch at Karmi.

The information they have is certainly shocking and unexpected. Hamza, not one to waste time, gets straight to the point.

'Victor Rotizki is dead.'

224

I look at him blankly.

'Otherwise known as Mr. V,' Ahmet adds.

I try and digest the information.

'Serious?'

'He was shot,' says Ahmet, looking proud to give me the information first hand. 'It's the name of his killer that's the bigger surprise.'

'Who was it?' I ask.

'Manov!' says Hamza.

It turns out that when the authorities released Manov Pavluk, he returned to the UK. But little did they know they were issuing a death ticket for Victor Rotizki. What a way to go: being murdered in cold blood by a member of your gang, on your doorstep.

It isn't long before the media picks up on the story, and it's all over the news. One paper in particular (the same one that previously labelled me a fugitive), highlights the fact Manov was in Northern Cyprus, where the ex-Luton footballer, Andrew Ashford, lives. The worst part of it is that there's nothing I can do about it as they have stated a fact- I am indeed here. Wisely they refrained from using words such as 'fugitive' or 'hiding-out', leaving it to the readers' imagination to decide if I had something to do with Victor's demise. And yes... they do link Victor to Lewis's- disappearance.

Luckily the police have already closed both the Rotizki and Orland cases. As far as they are concerned, Victor Rotizki exterminated Lewis Orland, and Manov Pavluk shot Rotizki.

Word has it Manov didn't even contact his family when returning to London. He hung around close to Rotizki's property in Hampstead and watched the building for almost two days- until he had a clear view of his target and its two guards. He shot all three men in the back of the head. It's unclear how he got hold of the 9mm semi-automatic, but he's thought to have bought- or borrowed- it from an old acquaintance.

Oddly, he didn't try to run or hide after committing the crimes. He just waited for the police to arrive at the scene and take him away- as if he wanted to show the world that he'd killed Rotizki.

A mixture of emotions hit me. I start to feel free, like finally being let out of a small cage. Just as well, as I am invited to the Alp residence for dinner this evening.

I enter my stuffy flat and call mother to tell her the news about Mr. V's death, but obviously, she's already read about it in the papers and also watched it on the news.

'When I saw his face on the front page, it was like he was still standing here in the living room with that sarcastic smirk on his face!' she retorts.

'Well, he isn't. It's over, mum. He's gone.'

'Your aunt's taken it worse. She's overwhelmed. It brought back bad memories.'

'Can't be easy. But it's over now.'

'I don't like speaking ill of the dead, but good!'

'I can't say he'll be missed by many.'

'Anyway dear, now that he's gone and the football season is over, when are you returning home?'

I pause for a moment, thinking about how delicately as possible I can word my next sentence.

'Mum, I am thinking of proposing to Aysha.'

She goes silent.

'Mum?'

'Oh… I see. That's great, dear,' she says eventually, not sounding at all pleased. 'Well, why don't you bring her here? I'd like to meet my future daughter in law.'

'That's another thing. As Dad is no longer with us, you must come and ask her father for her hand for me. It's how it's done here.'

'But doesn't she have a say in all this?'

'Of course, she does. That's why I'm going to propose first.'

'What if she says no?'

'Well, then there'd be no point in asking… why would she say no?'

She laughs and says she would be delighted, as long as I get both her and Anita's air tickets.

I sit directly opposite Alp, who's in his wheelchair. Sibel sits next to him and Aysha next to me. There's enough food on the large dining table to feed at least ten people. That's no exaggeration; Cypriots like a large variety of food on the table.

It's here I taste one of the best dishes since coming to the island. Sure, I've eaten dolma (stuffed vine leaves) on numerous occasions, but never before have I tried çiçek-dolması. Instead of wrapping the rice with vine leaves, the stuffing is wrapped with the flower of a pumpkin. Although they have a lady who helps with the cooking, Sibel claims she's cooked everything herself.

'Aysha just isn't interested in cooking,' she says, gently placing a spoonful of yogurt on her plate's edge. 'The new generation isn't in general.'

'I blame all the new takeaway places,' Alp adds. 'You get garbage delivered to your doorstep within twenty minutes.'

'That's not fair,' says Aysha, blushing. 'I make a great spaghetti bolognaise.'

'That, you do,' her father agrees.

After dinner, Turkish coffees are served, and Alp invites me to his study, while the ladies watch a Turkish TV show. His study is spacious. A large red Persian carpet covers most of the wooden floor. Behind his vintage desk, the distant Kyrenia lights glitter through a large window. Next to the desk is a hostess trolley with dark wooden trays, being held up by golden pillars, with delicate golden wheels beneath. Alp gets two short whisky-glasses out of the side cupboard and picks up one of the six whisky bottles.

'Ice?' he asks.

'Yes, please.'

He chucks in a couple of cubes in both the glasses, which I notice are both made of crystal. I wonder if he's even permitted to drink so soon after the operations.

He hands me the glass of whisky and tells me to take a seat. I get a sense that this will lead to something more. I am dating his daughter, and in this part of the world, I know that daughters aren't given away easily. He then opens the lid of the cigar-humidifier, which sits in the trolley's bottom tray and takes out two cigars.

'Robustos[17],' he says, cutting the ends with a cigar-cutter and handing one over.

I thank him and hold it up close. It's about six inches with a black and orange ring, displaying the name Cohiba in golden letters. He then passes me a cigar-lighter with three small blowtorch sections. Their flames are so intense they almost burn my eyebrows. Suddenly I feel a large puff of smoke rapidly entering my lungs, and I start to choke.

'Easy now. Cigars aren't meant to be inhaled,' Alp chuckles, amused and red-faced: not a side to him I've seen before.

He wheels himself next to the other visitor's chair on the other side of the small table and turns to face me. For a moment, his face disappears in a large cloud of smoke as he lights up, taking multiple puffs to get the cigar to burn evenly. When satisfied, he looks up at me, the dim lighting in the study revealing the large bags under his tired eyes.

---

[17] Robusto: Refers to the size of the cigar.

'So, Ashford, how's your first year here been?' he asks, with a slightly more serious tone.

'I certainly put more weight on, thanks to all the beautiful Cypriot food.'

He nods and smiles.

The football training here is less hours than that of professional clubs- a lot less- because most of the players have jobs. So, I've been burning fewer calories, but I decide to keep that comment to myself.

'I agree. It's difficult to keep away from the food here. So, now that Mr. V is dead. As your representative, have you decided on your next step?' he asks, looking deep into my eyes, searching for the answer before I give it to him.

'Yes sir, I have. I would like to stay on for another season. Maybe we can get two consecutive championships.'

Alp smiles and takes another large puff of the cigar.

'Sounds like music to my ears,' he says.

'So, Lewis has definitely been murdered by Mr. V,' he confirms quietly in almost a whisper, not quite sure himself whether he is asking a question or making a statement.

I slowly nod. 'Yes, although no evidence has been found.'

'No body?'

'No body. That's the most difficult part to accept. The uncertainty of it.'

'True.'

There's a short pause, while loud-speaking echoes from the TV down the corridor. Alp then directs the conversation away from Lewis and tells me about his life. He tells me how he met Sibel and how he came from a poor upbringing. I also tell him about parts of my childhood. I see some similarities even though we both grew up in different times and places. We both came from poverty and we both lost our fathers at a young age.

I look at the grandfather clock standing tall in the corner of the room. It reads eight minutes past eleven. I tilt back the glass and swallow the last drop of whisky, leaving half the Robusto to burn itself out in the ashtray.

'It's getting late. I don't want to keep you from going to bed,' I say.

'There's just one more thing before you go.'

I stay seated and look at him in full concentration.

'I see that you and Aysha are... enjoying each other's company. You've been dating for quite a while now. I just want to bring it to your attention. Here, we only go out with girls that we see a definite future with,' he says, with a slight smile.

I have no idea whether he means that as a friendly bit of advice or a threat, but I'm guessing the latter, if not both.

25

May 28th

AFTER searching almost every jewellery shop in town, I stumble upon a delicate-looking engagement ring just right for proposing to Aysha. Its elegant 14K white gold body and sizable round diamond, glittering under the store lights, draw me to it.

It's here I do something I'm not used to doing- I bargain! When I first arrived, I noticed a lot of haggling going on, in every corner- no doubt a tradition that primarily rubbed off from the mainland, on the once Anglicised island.

'Is that your final offer?' I ask the lady standing on the other side of the display table, trying to sound polite and as far from intimidating as possible.

At first, she looks slightly taken aback that someone English- possibly a tourist- would start to haggle, but then she keeps her composure and calmly answers, 'I'm afraid that ring is from our new season collection, so I cannot lower the price. However, if you'd like something a little more reasonable, sir, I can show you some rings from our sales collection over here.'

'Thank you, but I like this one,' I answer.

I end up paying the full amount and rush home to lock it up in the small safe hidden inside the back of the cupboard in the bedroom.

I call Ahmet, who gave me a good idea of how to propose. His cousin- who happens to be Mustafa Hamza's younger brother- is a pilot. If I pay for the fuel and banner, he will be happy to fly past with a message during the proposal. Not many opportunities arise for such proposals, although I do find the idea quite cheesy.

'Where and when are you thinking of doing it?' he asks.

'This Saturday at the Golden Beach in Karpaz,' I answer, hoping that his cousin will be available to fly on that day.

'Okay, I'll ask Sadık. Should be okay, I think, but you need to make sure the banner is ready by then,' he says.

'There's a printer on the way to Bellapais. They said they'd have it ready by Thursday.'

'Did you tell them what it's for?'

'Yes.'

'That's okay then. I'll check with Sadık and get back to you.'

'Thanks, Ahmet, much appreciated.'

Just after noon, while lost inside a TV show on *Flicks*, I receive a call from a man, with well-spoken English, who introduces himself as Özer.

'Mr. Ashford, please can we meet somewhere? I have a bonus payment to hand over to you,' he says.

'Really? Are you sure? I wasn't aware of further bonuses.'

'You are the Andrew Ashford, who played for Luton Town and is currently playing for Doğan Türk Birliği, are you not?'

'I am.'

'Then, I *am* sure. Would you prefer I'd come over to yours?'

'How about I pick it up from the club building?' I say, not wanting to invite a stranger over.

Having already received my bonuses, I start feeling suspicious.

'Best not to meet at the club,' he answers. 'This is a low-key side-payment if you see what I mean.'

'I really don't.'

At this point, alarm bells start going off in my head.

'How about we meet outside the 20 Temmuz Stadium?' he says.

At least that's public, I think to myself.

'Ok. When?'

'Two o'clock?'

'Two's fine,' I answer.

'Good. Make sure you come by car. It's not a good idea to walk the streets with all this cash on you.'

'Just how much are we talking about here?'

'One hundred and twenty thousand pounds.'

My jaw drops.

'One hundred and twenty thousand!'

It sounds too good to be true. Not even in England have I ever received a bonus payment as much as this. Perhaps it's directly from Alp and not the club. Maybe he's heard that I'm planning to propose to Aysha. Ahmet might have given him a heads-up. Or it's not that at all. It could be his way of thanking me for saving his life. Either way, there's only one way to find out.

The stadium is only a two-minute drive from the flat, so it probably wasn't a great idea to leave fifteen minutes early.

I've never heard Özer's name mentioned at the club. I even question whether he works for the club. Parking opposite the stadium's main entrance, I wait in the car, looking out for a man with possibly a briefcase or some kind of bag.

After sitting inside the car and browsing the news on social media, a white Honda eventually pulls up and parks, facing the Polo. A tanned man with shaved hair and sunglasses nods at me, then gets out the car.

'Hello Andrew, I'm Özer.' he says, as I approach him.

He holds a brown box, sealed with tape, the type used for storing things when moving houses.

'There must be some mistake. There was no mention of this in the contract. I already received a bonus last week. Did Hasan Alp arrange this?' I ask.

'Congratulations. You played a big part in making the team championships. Some would say single-handedly,' he says, ignoring the question. 'It's best you don't ask any questions. Or say anything to Alp either.'

'In that case, how will I know if this is an official payment?'

The question makes him slightly uncomfortable. He winces and rests the box on the bonnet of his car.

'You want to settle here in Cyprus, do you not? Maybe get married and start a family? Or a little business on the side? You're an athlete, Mr. Ashford, and I don't need to remind you that your value will go down with age. So, I recommend you take the money. I have a lot of things to do today, so I can't waste time!'

'Open it,' I say.

'Open it?' he repeats, surprised.

'Open the box and show me the cash.'

'All right,' he sniffs, scanning the area and signals for me to get closer to the car.

He drops the box onto the back seat, takes out a Swiss army knife, flicks it open, jabs it into the tape, tears it, and opens the box. I look inside, amazed to see that it's full of fifty-pound notes. They look so clean as if they've just been freshly printed. Taking out a stack- tied by an elastic band- I examine it.

'Okay, now you've done your security check, please take it and go,' says Özer, hastily.

I take the box from his car and watch him whiz away.

I rush home, debating where to store the cash without raising suspicion. I fill up the safe with as many notes as it can take. The rest- twenty thousand to be exact- I bring to the bank. The bank manager asks to see me, wondering where I got this much cash. I tell her it's a bonus from the club.

At first, she gives me a suspicious look.

Then says, 'Thank you, Mr. Ashford. The money has been credited to your account.'

26

BEING fortunate enough to play football at a professional level in the past, came with its advantages. It gave me the time and opportunity to travel to many countries around the world, not to mention visiting countless beaches. However, nothing has impressed me as much as the sea in Karpaz.

Geographically it is the most prominent piece of land on the island, pointing northeast towards eastern Turkey and Syria. Mainly, the place is known for two things- the immaculate long stretches of golden beaches with crystal clear blue waters- and secondly, its wild donkeys.

Aysha said I needed to experience Karpaz for myself. So here I am, on the road with her- driving along the north-eastern coast- taking in the flawless scenery and listening to her *latest hits'* playlist.

It takes a good two hours to arrive at one of her favourite beaches, which also has a restaurant further up the cliff overlooking the bay. Apparently, it's well known for its fresh fish and meze.

Today I will propose while swimming in the sea. Sadık got permission from the authorities to fly the Cessna 172 plane, with the banner that reads: Aysha Will You Marry Me?

Luckily, Sadık isn't new to flying banners, as he's previously flown a couple of advertisements for companies. We agree that the plane will fly over Golden Beach at 3 pm- the time I have to make sure I'm in the water with Aysha.

On the way to Karpaz, as we pass Alagadi (also known as Turtle Beach), *A Bar for Sale* sign catches my eye. The wooden hut, which is about two hundred metres away from the beach, has seen some better days- just by looking at it from the outside- it's evident it needs a lot of work. I start to dream of what it would be like to run a beach bar and mention it to Aysha. Being one who always likes living spontaneously, she smiles and says, 'Why not?'

Perhaps the mysterious bonus was an act of God (although I'm not at all religious). Maybe I'm destined to open up a small business, just like Özer said while handing over the money. From the sales sign, I save the estate agent's number to make some queries on Monday.

As we drive through Karpaz, I notice the land is untouched- no houses, no shops, and no developments- just beautiful bays with unpolluted waters. Here I begin to understand why it's a popular place for sea lovers and weekend getaways.

We come across a couple of wild donkeys. One is blocking the road, brave enough to think that no oncoming vehicles can ever run it over on this secluded piece of road. We stop, and to my surprise, it walks towards us- stopping at the driver's door- looking inside with tearful and imploring eyes. Aysha takes out carrots from her handbag, tied in a small plastic refrigerator-bag.

'I always come prepared,' she smiles, handing over a carrot.

'Wait, you want me to feed it?' I ask.

'Of course! Look at the way he's looking at you,' she replies, making her voice cute and baby-like.

I wind down the window. Heat gushes in and mixes with the cold air of the air-conditioning, instantly making it warmer inside the vehicle.

'Keep your palm flat. Unless you want to lose some fingers!' she warns.

'Nice.'

With a trembling hand, I reach out, giving the burro its snack, which it hoovers up in a gulp. Enjoying the moment, Aysha laughs as she takes a couple of pictures. It's not long before the other two donkeys join us. Within five minutes, all the carrots are gone, and we continue our journey. On the way, we come across more donkeys but are out of carrots.

Finally, we arrive at our destination, park the car at the secluded car park, and head straight to the restaurant for lunch. When the food starts coming, I see why Aysha spoke so highly of this place. The seafood meze is spot on, and the fish- although a little overcooked- is tasty.

A family runs the place. The wife barely comes out of the kitchen as she is continuously cooking; the husband is at the front line, and their two daughters wait on the tables.

We wash the food down with a cold Efes beer, occasionally staring out at the glittering water, stretching out to the horizon like a silk carpet.

I feel the box of the engagement ring digging into my leg, inside the pocket of my swimming trunks. Not long left. The plane should be flying past in about forty minutes- my heart races when I think about it.

I look deep into Aysha's eyes and ask her, 'If I was to return to the UK one day, would you come with me?'

She gives me a startled look and answers 'It depends.'

'On what?'

'Where we are in our relationship.'

'Okay.'

'But if we are in the right place, then I will stand by your side wherever you go,' she says.

I know what she means- or at least I think I do.

We finish eating and make our way down to the beach.

As it's the start of the summer, the beach is relatively quiet. Most of the locals start swimming in July and a lot of tourists- who mainly come from the UK- arrive in August.

We set our stuff down on a spot close to the water. Aysha removes her white T-shirt and denim shorts, stripping down to her blue bikini, revealing her perfectly toned body. I take off my shirt, trying not to reveal the ring box's outline, by covering my trunk's pocket with my hand.

Aysha is too busy to notice. She runs into the water.

'Come on!' she calls, splashing water towards me.

I follow her, kicking the hot sand with every stride until I feel the cold water covering my feet.

'I'll race you to the buoys,' she challenges, with an almost perfect front crawl.

'That's not fair! You have a head start!' I call after her, laughing at her daredevilry after seeing how far the buoys are.

It's these little things about her I love- how she makes every moment dramatic and fun- and very soon, I will be giving her a choice- until death does us part.

After a short while, my body adapts to the cold water. She won't admit to it, but the race finishes a draw.

Suddenly, I panic. The box isn't in my pocket. Aysha notices the horror in my face.

'What is it? Did you see something under the water?' she asks with a trembling voice. 'A great white was spotted at the Pan Handle, in Karpaz. It was in the news last December.'

'No, everything's fine,' I say, trying to keep the panic in my voice to a minimum.

I look down into the deep water below, never before in my life seeing the sea so clear as this, with many colours reflecting on the sandy depth. How glad I am that it is clear. A school of tiny fish races past, as below a hermit crab lazily crawls on a bit of rock- but the navy box bearing the engagement ring is nowhere to be seen.

It will have the same destiny as the one in the Titanic movie, I think to myself.

Except this is not a movie and certainly wasn't intentional.

With panic, I swim back- retracing my steps- worried the plane will fly past any second.

Without the ring, the proposal would be a disaster- one that I won't be able to put on hold- because of the banner on the plane writing Aysha's name would be a give-away.

'Are you sure you're okay?' she asks.

'Yes! Fine!' I reply, like a hawk scanning every inch of the sea below.

'Oh my God, you got stung by a jellyfish, haven't you? There are swarms of them during May and June!'

'Do I look like I'm in pain?'

'Kind of. But seriously, what is it?'

It's at that moment I hear buzzing- the buzzing engines of the Cessna 172 jet. With desperation, I search harder and faster, swimming back towards the shore.

I spot a shadow and lunge towards it. But it's the shadow of a piece of stone, so I end up grabbing a handful of sand. Before heading back up, I notice something else close by, dancing with the tide below.

With a last desperate attempt, gasping for breath, I swim closer to the object. It is indeed the box! I grab it and lightheadedly rocket back up to the surface.

When my head's out the water, I see Aysha looking up at the passing plane, flying directly above us. She covers her blushing cheeks as she treads water.

I open the box before her stunned gaze, exposing the ring, which under the bright summer sun, appears more blinding than before. The plane turns and heads back west, disappearing over the mountains, with the banner noisily flapping behind it.

Getting my breath back, I ask, 'Will you be my wife?'

She looks a deep meaningful look into my eyes, 'Yes,' she breathes with a smile.

I feel a huge weight lifting off my shoulders. Removing the ring from the box, I delicately place it onto her ring finger, taking a sigh of relief that it fits perfectly.

'It's beautiful,' she says softly.

'Yes, it is.'

'Hang on. Did you fish it from under the water?'

'Don't ask,' I answer with a smile.

'And the plane… cheesy, but sweet.'

'Bet you weren't expecting that.'

'You certainly caught me off guard.' she says, checking out the diamond on her finger.

She presses her naked skin against mine and we kiss- a kiss that tastes of the sea- our bodies tremble with excitement. And this time I don't go after the box, which has probably made its way to the bottom by now.

When we return to Kyrenia late evening, I call my mother to tell her the good news: *Although the proposal was dramatic, she still said yes.*

With excitement in her voice, she says, 'Congratulations, dear. So, shall Anita and I start packing?'

'Good idea! Your flight is on Friday.'

June 3ʳᵈ

The following day I force myself out of bed, feeling sore thanks to my sunburnt shoulders. I call the estate agent to enquire about the beach bar for sale.

'Hello, this is Tara speaking, how can I help?' answers a female voice on the other end.

'Hello, I want to ask about the old beach bar for sale at Alagadi.'

'You mean The Old Windmill Beach Bar.'

'Yes, that's the one.'

'You're in luck. This one's going for cheap.'

'How come?'

'The owners put it up for sale and had to rush off to Australia. Family emergency.'

'How much are they asking?' I ask.

'Seventy thousand pounds.'

Bargain! Maybe too good to be true! I tell myself. *Keep calm and don't show your excitement…*

'When can I have a look inside?'

'This afternoon at two okay?'

'That's perfect.' I reply.

Perfect indeed…

27

1 Year Later

WHAT a year it's turned out to be, I think to myself, as I sit on a table at the far end of The Windmill Beach Bar (a name I decided not to change), doing the accounts.

So much can happen in a year, and yet time flies in the blink of an eye. The wedding which was held at Bellapais Abbey in late September now seems a distant memory. It was only a small event, with just family and close friends. Aysha chose to invite as few people as possible, which didn't include most of her relatives (and trust me she has lots). To this day, some still aren't talking to her (or her parents). It's a sore subject for the Alps, one they'd rather not discuss, Aysha on the other hand, couldn't give a monkey's.

Mum and Aunt Anita arrived on Friday and tried their best to fit in at the Alp residence, on the eve of the *"asking."* Mum's attempt to impress the Alps by trying to speak Turkish was just about bearable; Anita getting drunk, and loud and flirting with Hasan's younger brother, wasn't.

Falling in love with the place (as many do on their first visit), mum ended up moving into the house in Karmi and made quite a few friends. Anita however, went back to England and promised she'd visit us every summer.

Aysha and I moved into a house on the outskirts of Bellapais, after a two-week honeymoon in Cuba (One we both wished had never ended). Surrounded by a large green garden with a fair-sized swimming pool, the house is a perfect place to raise a family.

It's been another successful year, with Doğan winning the league for a second successive season. On a personal note, the biggest success was getting through an entire year without a single injury. However, I reached a tough decision to retire from the game altogether, after a long and heated meeting with Alp, who is still against the idea.

Lewis is still missing. I often think about him. Word has it that the search for him has ended. Both the Spanish and British authorities agreed that the arson attack killed him. He was finally declared dead a couple of months ago, even though no body has been recovered.

And then there is The Windmill Beach Bar…

The place has proven to be a hit with the ex-pats, as well as the Turkish Cypriots. The burgers and the fish and chips are a hit, but the Sunday roast steals the show.

Aysha walks out of the kitchen, her pregnant belly poking through her loose pink T-shirt.

'The beef patties are ready, and in the fridge,' she says breathlessly.

'You should really be resting,' I say. 'I'll be fine. Seran is here.'

'I'm pregnant, not disabled. Plus, Seran is peeling the potatoes for the chips. She can't do everything.'

Aysha certainly has a point. Another helper will be necessary, now that she has to rest before the birth.

'We'll definitely need an extra pair of hands at the weekends,' I say, putting down the pen.

'Maybe Nalan can help. She's free at the weekends.'

'If she doesn't mind helping for a couple of hours during the lunches, that'll be great,' I say.

'I'll ask her,' Aysha replies; as I pull out a chair, slowly guiding her to sit down.

I sit back down and look at her from across the table. The pregnancy certainly hasn't changed her. If I didn't know she was pregnant, I'd be none the wiser. She hasn't put on any extra pounds around the face, body, or limbs and looks prettier than ever. In fact, the only way to tell she's pregnant is by looking at her from the side.

Apologetically she says, 'You're sure you'll be okay?'

'I'll manage,' I say as I lean over and give her a peck on the lips. 'Plus, Berk is here.'

'Berk is nine. Last week he started playing football in the yard with the customers.'

'I suppose he's providing entertainment,' I say with a smile. 'Talk of the devil.'

Berk walks in wearing a white Real Madrid shirt, pale blue swimming trunks, and red Spiderman flip-flops. He's Seran's son, and after a swim at the beach every Saturday, his father drops him here.

'Hello Berkie' I say, as he walks past.

He grins a big grin, revealing his missing front teeth, as he walks into the kitchen to report to his mum.

The front door swings open and in walk the first set of customers- followed by more- as the bar starts filling up. Again, Aysha insists she will help, but I tell her to go. Seran hurries out of the kitchen and starts taking orders. I attend to a couple seated at the other end.

'How can I help you?' I ask.

'I'll have the Windmill Cheeseburger,' says the man.

'Is the cod fresh?' asks his other half.

'All cod is frozen.'

'Really? And why is that?' she asks, smugly.

'Cod can only be found in the North Sea,' I reply, calmly.

A gentleman wearing a baseball cap and large black sunglasses covering most of his face is wheeled in by his wife/carer. As Seran and I are both busy, Berk jumps to the rescue and holds the door open. When they are through, he shows them to one of the tables closer to the bar, but the elderly gentleman on the wheelchair signals to the table closest to the front door. At least I assume he is elderly. I notice something strange about his face. It seems scarred like he's had a fight with a cat. I'd say the lady is in her mid to late forties and looks good for her age. I notice some of the men on the other tables staring at her.

'I'll be with you shortly,' I tell them.

The man in the wheelchair nods back in approval.

'So, the fish is frozen then,' the lady whose order I'm taking continues.

'I'm afraid so.'

She thinks for a moment and replies, 'Just a cheese salad. And make it quick!'

Occasionally a rude customer walks in, but I'm okay with that, having come out the other side of the dog-eat-dog world of football and surviving.

As I walk towards the kitchen to place the orders, I notice Berk attending the table with the man in the wheelchair and the lady.

'What would you like to drink?' he asks them politely with his broken English.

'Hello, young man,' whispers the man in the wheelchair breathlessly, struggling to project his voice. 'Two lemonades, please.'

'So how come you're in a wheelchair?' asks Berk- curiosity getting the better of him.

'Berk! That's rude!' intervenes Seran. 'I'm sorry-'

'That's okay,' laughs the man. 'Your boy's upfront. I like that.'

Seran nods with a shy smile.

He then casts his attention back on Berk. 'You see kiddo; I'm in a wheelchair because my legs aren't as strong as they once were. I got hurt because I wasn't good.'

Berk looks at him in bewilderment. 'I always try to be good,' he says.

'Now, there's a good boy.'

More customers walk in and place themselves at the vacant tables. Seran quickly jots down two Caesar salads and two lemonades and rushes into the kitchen.

I hurry to the bar to fix those drinks. Running around the busy restaurant like a headless chicken, making sure all tables get their food and drink certainly feels more tiring than a ninety-minute football game. I then rush into the kitchen, carefully placing a cheese slice on a beef patty, covering the top with the upper bun, then throw some chips next to it.

Rushing back out, I make my way to the table at the far centre and serve the cheeseburger. On the way back, the man in the wheelchair looks up from his Caesar salad and forces a misshaped smile.

'Hope you're enjoying your salads,' I say.

'Oh, very much so. The taste buds don't work like they used to, but I'm enjoying it,' he says. 'I like what you've done with this place.'

'Thank you. Sorry for the slow service today. My wife usually helps, but she's pregnant.'

'Congratulations! When's she due?'

'We're expecting in December.'

'That's fantastic! Is it a boy or a girl?'

'It's a boy.'

He looks at the lady, who doesn't say a word. He then looks back at me and smiles.

'So happy for you. Make the most of what you have,' he says. I feel his focused glance behind the dark sunglasses.

'Thank you,' I say, not quite sure of what he means.

But judging by his condition, I debate with myself whether he's 'all there'.

'Enjoy your meals,' I say and get back to work, to make sure the last couple of tables get served.

'Thank you,' he calls from behind as I walk away.

The bar empties with only one table left. They'd already paid but casually sit finishing off their drinks. I open the till and place the notes inside. Seran walks up to me, takes out a white envelope from her overall's pocket, and hands it over.

'What's this?' I ask, noticing my name written on it.

'I found it under the salt holder on table six.'

'When?'

'Just now.'

'I wonder what it is,' I say.

Seran shrugs.

'Who was sitting on table six?' then I remember exactly who it was- the man in the wheelchair and the silent lady.

'Whoever they were, they knew you,' Seran tells me, before heading to the kitchen to mop the floor- and leaving me with the envelope.

I tear it open, removing a piece of paper from inside and unfolding it. I start feeling lightheaded even before I begin to read it. Straightaway, I recognize the handwriting.

Dear Andy!

I knew you wouldn't recognize me! I don't blame you. You were extremely busy and let's face it, I am not as handsome as I once was. To be honest, I hardly recognize myself either.

Daphne takes good care of me though, with a handsome pay, of course, otherwise, she wouldn't look at me twice. She sees my every need if you know what I mean.

Andy, my old friend, call this is a letter of apology if you will. You should know that all my actions were in your best interest, even if it meant you getting injured in the first game of the season.

I have another confession, and you can thank me for this one, I sabotaged your engagement with Jessie Fell, as she would have ruined the plan.

Obviously, she wasn't right for you. Even Pablo thought twice about sleeping with her when I paid him.

I'm proud of you, Andy. Aysha is a good catch. The wedding was certainly a joyful occasion and yes, I was there.

I see you invested the money wisely. The Windmill certainly has character, and your cooking isn't too bad either.

At the end of the day, it all worked out, although destiny has punished me.

I have no name or face anymore, and will always live hidden in the shadows.

I hope someday you'll find it in yourself to forgive me.
Your old friend,
Lewis.

I stare at the letter, fighting back the tears, with a mixture of emotions, then I rush into the kitchen.

'Did the man in the wheelchair pay cash or card?', I ask Seran, hoping for the cardholder's name.

'He paid cash,' she answers, mopping the floor. 'They'd left by the time I brought back the change.'

'Did you see what they were driving?'

'No.'

'Any mention where they were headed, or where they're staying? Anything at all?' I ask in desperation.

'Sorry,' she replies, placing the mop inside the cupboard. 'They just disappeared.'

I cover my face with my hands and take a deep breath. How can I ever find it in myself to forgive him? I think of Aysha.

Authors Note

It has always been my dream to write a novel that involves a unique love story, as well as an introduction to the culture and history of Northern Cyprus. As in many countries around the world, football is the main sport in Cyprus, a sport that brings people with a common bond together.

All the locations, hotels, restaurants, cafes and the football teams in this novel are real.

The embargo preventing Northern Cyprus football teams to participate in FIFA competitions continues to this day. The references that are used regarding the past politics between the Cyprus Turkish Football Association and FIFA have been taken from past researches and recordings. I have tried to keep them as accurate as possible.

N.K. Chavush

7 April 2020

Printed in Great Britain
by Amazon

56460306R00158